FINAL CHAPTERS

Book FOUR of the Shane Davison Chronicles

A NOVEL in THREE PARTS

Dale Thele

Book Four
Shane Davison Chronicles

Published by

Fountain Literary Press
a unique approach to publishing

Austin, Texas, USA

Copyright © 2024 by Dale Thele

ISBN 979-8-9857557-4-9   (Paperback)
ISBN 979-8-9857557-5-6   (Kindle)

First Digest Paperback Printing: March 4, 2024

ASIN B0CX4WP876

13 14 15 16 33 23 24 25 26 24

DISCLAIMER

This is a work of fiction. Although inspired by actual events, the reader should not assume any portion of this manuscript is factual. In addition, this manuscript is a period piece taking place from Thursday, June 10, 1982 to Saturday, December 15, 1984. Being that this is a period piece, some terms and phrases may be considered outdated, or inappropriate for the present day. Use of terms and words are intended to give a sense of authenticity and should not be deemed racial, or intended to be hateful, or belittling by today's social standards. Be aware of the use of profanity, drug and alcohol use, homophobia, homosexuality; you the reader are hereby forewarned.

Characters in this manuscript, although they may have similarities to persons living or dead, are purely accidental. The principal location where this story takes place is real, however other references may be creations of the author.

All scenes, dialog, characters, and story settings are products of the author's imagination and are not to be construed as factual. Other than stated, any resemblance to actual persons, living or dead, events, businesses, and locales are altogether coincidental.

*"Even if you cannot change all the people around you,
you can change the people you choose to be around.
Life is too short to waste your time on people
who don't respect, appreciate, and value you.
Spend your life with people who make you smile,
laugh, and feel loved."*

~ Roy T. Bennett ~
The Light in the Heart

"Writing a book eventually leads to having to write the final chapter."

~ Dale Thele ~

PART ONE

CAROUSEL PONIES

Thursday, June 10, 1982

"Life is a carousel.
It goes up and down.
All U gotta do is just stay on."

~ Pharrell Williams ~

The year is 1982. Ronald Reagan is President of the United States. In January, Ozzy Osbourne bit the head off a bat on stage in Des Moines, Iowa. In March, the Doobie Brothers, a rock group, split up after twelve years. Also, in the same month, groundbreaking began in Washington, D.C., for the Vietnam Veterans Memorial. In April, Sally Ride became the first female astronaut. Dr. Michael E. DeBakey performed the first successful heart transplant in the U.S.A. The number one Billboard single in the U.S.A. was Olivia Newton-John's "Physical".

While those and other events may have been newsworthy, they aren't the story I'm about to tell you. My humble story takes place in Austin, the capital city of the Great State of Texas, home of the University of Texas. The city boasts a population of 415,000, and I've lived here for the past six years.

So much has happened to me in those six years; it's hard to believe. First, I've aged a bit; my hair has thinned slightly, and my waistline is a little thicker. But that's not all—I've started a new chapter in my life. I've made some incredible friends and learned valuable life lessons. I'm happy with the life I've made for myself. Unfortunately, a few years back, things took a turn for the worse when, in the spring, Momma was diagnosed with cancer. It hit me hard just as the grass and trees were turning green. Before I knew it, the autumn leaves started falling and Momma was gone. Watching her deteriorate right before my eyes was incredibly tough, and it happened so fast, too. The hardest part, though, was that I didn't take action to resolve our differences before she passed. Time slipped away, just like she did in her sleep one autumn night.

Shortly after her diagnosis, when she first fell ill, and in what felt like the blink of an eye, she was hooked up to life support machines. Towards the end, I have no clue if she even recognized me or heard my voice. She just lay there, still, with her eyes closed, almost as if she were sleeping. Each day, she grew weaker and lost more weight. The cancer ravaged her until there was barely anything left. It was heartbreaking to see her like that. In the end, she was unrecognizable. I wished for her suffering to end. I know it sounds cruel, but I hoped her heart would give out. She had been a good woman and didn't deserve to suffer. It was unbearable to witness her in such a state, knowing there was no chance of recovery.

Looking back, I regret not contacting her sooner, long before she fell ill. But my foolish pride got in the way, and then it was too late. She was taken from me far too soon, and I wasn't prepared for her to go.

As for me, I have a boyfriend. He and I recently took the plunge and bought an expensive downtown condo. It just made financial sense for us to live together rather than apart. So, he sold his suburban house, and I bid farewell to my leased southside condo. Together, we purchased our very own luxury condo. Did I mention that he's a super successful investment banker? I work as a financing broker. Talk about a power couple. And our offices are located in the financial district of downtown, near our condo, making our daily commute a breeze. We walk to our jobs.

I bet you're curious about my boyfriend and dying to know more about him. Well, let me spill the tea. We actually met a few years ago, thanks to mutual friends. At the time, I already had a boyfriend, so I didn't think much of Kip (my current beau) as potential boyfriend material. But, as life happened, things went south with my then-boyfriend, and I found myself single again. To make a long story short, a brief time later, Kip and I started dating. And let me tell you, it's been like living in a fairytale ever since.

Now that you have a glimpse into my world let me take you back to the morning when my perfect storybook life came crashing down in the most horrific way possible.

CHAPTER 1

Thursday morning, June 10
Kip's and my downtown condo

The day starts like any other weekday morning. We're going about our usual routines before heading to work, nothing unusual. I'm in the kitchen preparing breakfast, while Kip takes a shower in the master bathroom.

The doorbell rings.

Drying my hands with a dish towel, I head to the living room to answer the door.

It's Kip's son, Joshua, and his best friend, Dexter. I've known Dexter for about five years now. I suppose a little backstory would be helpful. You see, I used to work with Dexter's mom at Dillinger's department store before I became a financing broker. She introduced me to her two sons, Dexter and his older brother, Trent. From the get-go, Dexter took a shine to me. Even though he was just a kid of nine or ten at the time, he referred to me as his *adopted* uncle. Although Dexter and I weren't actually related in any way whatsoever, we became good friends.

Fast forward four years, and that's when I met Joshua, Dexter's friend. Soon after, I also got to know Joshua's dad, Kip. Now, I know this might not be the most pressing information, but it's worth mentioning that Dexter is gay, while Joshua is straight. But here's the thing—sexual orientation doesn't matter to any of us. Kip, me, and Dexter are cool with Joshua being the token straight in the family.

Speaking of the boys, I should stop referring to them as *boys*. Both are 18 years old and studying at the University of Texas. They're sharing a three-bedroom apartment close to campus, but here's the funny part—they have a roommate they hardly ever see. He's like this phantom roommate who vanishes into thin air. But honestly, none of us really care. Everything is—as the kids say: *copacetic*—as long as the roommate pays his share of the rent on time.

That's the skinny on Joshua and Dexter. They're just a couple of college kids navigating their way through life, and I'm lucky they've included me as their honorary *Uncle Shane*.

So, back to the boys rushing in the condo door and past me.

"Is breakfast ready?" Dexter asks, sniffing the air, most likely trying to guess what's on today's menu besides bacon.

"Coffee," Joshua says. "I need coffee." Like a zombie seeking brains, he follows the smell of freshly brewed coffee into the kitchen.

According to Kip, Joshua has never been much of a morning person, unlike Dexter. Dexter leaps out of bed, ready to tackle the day, just like I was at his age. However, I've outgrown that phase, thank goodness. Now, I'm more like Joshua. If given the chance, I could probably sleep all day, but with all the things I have to do every day, that's a luxury I can't afford.

"Where's dad?" Joshua asks, pouring freshly brewed coffee into a mug.

"He'll be out in a bit," I say. "He's in the shower."

"Hey, Uncle Shane, do you have any orange juice?" Dexter asks, searching the inside of the fridge.

"Look on the door shelf," I say. "There's a full pitcher."

"Thanks, I got it," Dexter says, shutting the fridge door with a quick kick of his foot. He then opens an over counter cabinet door and grabs a tall drinking glass.

"Josh?" Dexter asks while holding the cabinet door open. "You want a glass of juice?"

"No, I'm fine with my coffee," Joshua says, blowing on his mug of hot brew.

"Suit yourself," Dexter says, slamming the cabinet door shut. He hums to himself as he pours a glass of juice. Once the glass is full, he sets the juice container on the counter and takes a swallow from his glass. Crossing the kitchen, he takes a seat beside Joshua at the breakfast nook. I come behind Dexter, putting the juice container back inside the fridge. I've learned that asking the boys to return the juice in the refrigerator is pointless. They never listen. It's easier to do it myself rather than waste energy trying to convince them to do it. Gee wiz, I'm starting to sound like a mother hen.

"Uncle Shane, what's for breakfast?" Dexter asks.

"What are you in the mood for?" I ask while placing additional raw bacon slices in the sizzling hot skillet.

"Pancakes," Dexter says.

"No time for pancakes," Joshua says. "Dex, we've got that psych exam today. Pancakes are out of the question."

"Okay," Dexter says disappointedly. "I'll settle for a toaster pop-tart." He jumps up from the breakfast nook and begins rummaging through my pantry.

"Uncle Shane?" Dexter asks, ransacking my organized cabinet. "Don't you have a box of pop-tarts in all this stuff?"

"I think there's a box on the second—"

"Got 'em," Dexter interrupts, ripping open a new, unopened box of individually wrapped pastries."

The doorbell rings.

"Who can that be at this hour?" I ask.

"Want me to get it, Uncle Shane?" Joshua asks, jumping up from the breakfast nook.

"Do you mind?" I ask, turning hissing bacon in a skillet of hot grease.

Joshua goes to the front door.

Dexter wolfs down a pop-tart like he hasn't eaten in ages. However, I know that's not the case since he and Joshua had supper here last night. The two had hearty servings and even finished the chocolate cake I was lucky to snag from the nearby bakery. Those boys eat enough in a week to feed a small country for a month.

I hear voices from the living room, but I don't recognize them, nor can I make out what's being said.

7

"Josh, who's at the door?" I holler from the kitchen.

He appears in the kitchen doorway, visibly shaken and pale.

"Who's at the door?" I ask.

"They want my dad," a stunned Joshua says.

"Who wants your dad?" I ask, wiping my hands on a dish towel.

"A couple of cops..." Joshua answers.

"Did you say cops?" Dexter asks with wide eyes and untoasted pop-tart crumbs tumbling from his gaping mouth.

"Did I hear someone say something about the cops?" Kip asks, entering the kitchen with a beaming smile while adjusting his necktie.

"Yeah, Dad," Joshua says. "There's two of them, and they asked for you."

"Oh. I know. I bet it's about the upcoming Policeman's Ball," Kip nods. "We want two tickets? Right babe?" he gives me a glancing kiss as he crosses through the kitchen on his way to the living room.

"Of course," I nod.

Since Kip and I've been together, we've supported the annual fundraising event. We look forward to it every year.

Relieved the unexpected commotion has been settled, I remove crisp bacon strips from the frying pan and spread them on a paper towel-lined platter.

Kip greets the cops patiently waiting at the open front door with checkbook and ballpoint pen in hand.

"Good morning, officers," Kip says with a smile. "Come in, you don't need to stand out there in the hall. My, my, my, how time flies. It doesn't seem like it's already time for the annual Policeman's Ball. Shane and I'll take our usual two tickets. What do I owe you?" Kip holds a ballpoint pen ready to make out the check.

"Mr. Benson? Christopher Douglas Benson?" the first officer asks.

"Yes, that's me. There's no need to be so formal. You can call me Kip," he says, holding the checkbook open. "How much do I make this check for?"

"Mr. Benson," the first officer says. "You misunderstand. We're not selling tickets."

"I don't understand..."

"You're under arrest, Mr. Benson," the first officer says.

"What?" Kip asks, alternately searching the faces of the two cops. "Is this some kind of joke?"

"No, sir," the first officer says. "Please turn around, wrists together."

Kip does as he's told without hesitation.

The second officer cuffs Kip and then pats him down.

"Babe," Kip hollers. "Can you come here?"

Noticing Kip's strange tone, I wipe my hands on a tea towel and rush to the living room.

A curious Dexter and Joshua are on my heels.

We stop as we turn the corner from the kitchen to enter the living room. I'm stunned, seeing my lover and life partner in handcuffs.

Dexter and Joshua freeze on either side of me.

Never, in all my life, have I imagined I'd ever see my partner handcuffed like a common criminal.

"What's going on?" I demand.

"These officers are arresting me," Kip says.

"What are the charges?" I demand.

"Embezzlement, money laundering, fraud, and that's for starters," the first officer says.

"Babe, call Jim," Kip says. "Tell him to do whatever it takes to get this mess straightened out."

"Who's Jim?" Joshua asks.

"James Hanson," I say. "Your dad's and my attorney."

As Kip is escorted out of our condo by the second officer, his hands restrained by handcuffs, the other officer speaks up, ensuring Kip is aware of his rights.

"You have the right to remain silent..." the officer says, his voice firm yet composed. "You also have the right to an attorney. If you can't afford one, an attorney will be appointed

9

to represent you..."

Joshua, Dexter, and I follow the police officers to the door. Peering through the open doorway, we watch Kip being escorted down the hall away from our condo towards the elevator.

Kip glances back at us while the officers guide him into the elevator. His teary eyes meet mine as he's turned to face the empty hall he just walked through. His expression resembles a bewildered puppy, evoking a surge of emotion that brings hot tears to my eyes.

I tightly embrace the boys, my arms trembling, as Kip vanishes behind the closing elevator doors.

CHAPTER 2

Thursday afternoon, June 10
Kip's and my condo

"Yes, Jim, I understand," I say into the phone. "Thanks again, Jim. Call me if there are any new developments," I say. Puzzled. I hang up the phone.

"What did he say?" Joshua asks.

"Bail has been denied. The judge ruled your dad a flight risk," I repeat what Jim told me.

"What does that mean?" Joshua asks.

"The judge thinks your dad might leave town if he's granted bail," I say.

"That's ridiculous. Just who does that judge think my dad is?" Joshua says. "Dad wouldn't do that."

"I know that," I say. "You know that. Jim knows it, but the judge doesn't know your dad. No matter what we think, Jim says the judge isn't budging on granting bail."

"What else did Jim say?" Dexter asks.

"Well, the investment firm Kip works for filed the charges. One of the investment bankers claims Kip stole from the firm."

"That's bullshit," Joshua says.

"There's more," I say. "The guy who pointed a finger at your dad says he has indisputable proof Kip is guilty."

"No way," Joshua protests while angrily pacing.

"Jim suspects that someone is framing your dad," I repeat what Jim told me over the phone. "Jim also suspects that someone with deep pockets may have paid off the judge— concerning the bail denial. He can't prove it, but he's looking into it."

"What the—" Joshua says. "Why would someone do that to my dad?"

"I have no idea," I say, shaking my head.

"Maybe something else is going on?" Dexter says.

"Well, that's a possibility," I say. "Jim said he's wondering if the investment firm isn't using your dad as a distraction to cover up something much larger."

"You mean someone wants Mr. Benson to go down as the patsy?" Dexter asks.

"That's a real possibility," I say, shaking my head.

Joshua and Dexter ditch their classes for the day. Can you blame them for not wanting to attend class under these circumstances? I know what you're thinking—it's June; shouldn't they be on summer break? Well, here's the deal: the boys were initially starting college this coming fall. Instead, they decided to knock out a few required courses during the summer session. Why the summer session? Well, the summer classes are faster-paced due to limited time. They figured they could get a couple of classes out of the way during the shorter summer session rather than taking them in the fall semester.

The boys wasted no time; they jumped into their first summer classes at the university. Yet, I worry that they might burn out by not taking a break from classes during the summer. Unfortunately, there's no changing their minds once they've made a decision. Not only are they bullheaded, but those boys are also inseparable, always doing everything together. They've been like two peas in a pod since they were kids, or so I've heard from Dexter's mom and Kip. Did I tell you that Dexter and Joshua grew up just a few houses apart as kids? They've been best pals since before they could walk. Or, so I've been told. Now, that's a strong bond of friendship, if you ask me.

CHAPTER 3

Saturday, November 6
my condo

The sweltering summer months of June and July dragged on slowly, like a lazy box turtle. Unfortunately, there hasn't been any good news about Kip. Then, in August, came Kip's trial. Jim didn't expect it to come up so quickly, but it did. A jury of his peers found Kip guilty. It was no surprise, really. The prosecution spun so many lies and fabricated evidence against Kip that he didn't stand a chance of a fair trial. The whole ordeal made me sick to my stomach. After being bombarded with the prosecution's nonsense about Kip, no jury in their right mind would give Kip a get-out-of-jail-free card. Jim attempted to clear Kip's name, but he hit brick walls no matter where he turned. Jim strongly believed that some wealthy individual was hell-bent on framing Kip for the crime.

Kip's trial was a total sham, like one of those kangaroo courts you hear about. It was like the firm Kip dedicated almost two decades of his life had set out to destroy him. Can you believe it? Kip helped build that firm from the ground up, making it a successful and respected business. And now they look down on him like he's a criminal. The whole situation is mind-boggling, you know?

Who has a motive to do this to Kip? Who within the firm he was so loyal to suddenly turn and paint him as the bad guy? What's their reasoning behind making an innocent man like Kip into a big-time crook? Or is the firm hiding something? Is throwing Kip under the bus their way of protecting the firm's dark secrets? So many questions, but no answers. That's what's driving me crazy about the whole legal mess.

After the trial, Kip was sent up the river to the Texas State Penitentiary in Huntsville, Texas. The judge slapped him with a fifty-year sentence with no chance of parole. Jim thinks the punishment is way too harsh; it doesn't fit the fabricated crimes. He's convinced that someone is manipulating the whole damn judicial system. Jim's on a mission to uncover the corruption and won't rest until he discovers the truth. It's clear as day that someone went to great lengths to frame Kip and to keep him quiet. Being locked up for fifty years will keep him quiet, but does Kip really know anything? I don't think he knows squat. There's one silver lining in all this mess, though—at least no one's bumped Kip off to silence him. Then again, you never know what kind of shady shit might go down behind the walls of a century-old Texas prison.

The first Saturday in November is our *thing*, Kip and I. We looked forward to attending the annual Policeman's Ball. But that changed when Kip was carted away to the state penitentiary. Despite my reservations, I bought a single ticket for the event. If for nothing else, it's for a good cause. I'm not particularly interested in going, especially without Kip. The ball has a different theme every year; this year, it's a masquerade party. The idea intrigues me, but I know the event won't be as enjoyable without Kip.

However, Joshua and Dexter insist I go, if only to honor Kip. They think it's time for me to move on with my life. But I still love Kip too much to let him go. The boys remind me of that old saying, *When you fall off a horse, you've got to get right back on it*. But I'm not ready to get back on that horse, at least not yet. It's been four long months without Kip, and I have another forty-nine years and eight months to go before he's released. If I did the math correctly, I'll be seventy-three years old when Kip gets paroled. That's an incredibly long time to wait for someone. The odds are against us that one or both of us will live that long.

The boys may be right, though. Maybe I should move on

with my life. Forty-nine years and eight months is an awfully long time to put everything on hold for someone. No matter how much I love them.

I'm noncommittal with the boys about my going to the ball. I let them think that I'm not going to the annual event. Actually, I didn't convince myself to go till the last minute.

Arriving at the masquerade ball, I'm wearing a rented swashbuckler costume. For safety reasons, I left the accompanying sword at home. My face is concealed by a mask adorned with sparkling jewels, revealing only my eyes and mouth. I show up fashionably late and stand alone on the sidelines, observing the event with minimal enthusiasm, not in the mood to join the festivities.

I've been at the event for about an hour when I figure it's time to go home. Besides, I've made my obligatory appearance, and honestly, I'm not feeling the festive spirit. Just as I turn to leave, someone taps me on the shoulder.

Turning around, I come eye-to-eye with a man dressed in a costume very much like mine. He, too, is wearing a fancy mask covering his face. Without saying a word, he gestures for me to join him on the dance floor.

To be completely honest, I believe this guy has mistaken me for another partygoer. It's understandable, considering the similarity of our costumes and masks. Swashbuckler seems to be the popular go-to costume of the night. I shake my head, feeling uninterested in the party and dancing. Moreover, I've already made up my mind to go home.

Persistent, he takes my hand and leads us to the dance floor. Once there, he takes the lead in a waltz. He's an incredible dancer, way better than me, and completely outshines Kip by a mile.

A couple of years ago, Kip and I had a wild idea of enrolling in dance classes at a reasonably new, trendy dance studio. We were determined to become dance pros like Fred Astaire and

Ginger Rogers. But, for some reason, we never made it happen. Let's say neither of us had a natural talent for dancing. Honestly, we were awful—we stunk. But that didn't stop us from having a blast at charity dance events. We paired our four left feet together and danced the night away, only with each other, of course. We couldn't care less what others thought of our uncoordinated moves. All that mattered was that we were having a good time. Because, really, isn't that the whole point of attending these events? Supporting a good cause while having a darn good time?

Returning to the present Policeman's Ball, the stranger and I dance and dance. I lose count of the dances we shared without a break. As I gaze into the eyeholes of the stranger's mask, I'm captivated by his mesmerizing, dark eyes and lashes. His exposed, radiant smile lights up the entire room—pardon the cliché. I feel an irresistible draw towards him, longing to peek at what I imagine to be an incredibly handsome face lurking under that mask.

Surprisingly, I'm having a blast, especially when he leans in and kisses me. Luckily, I'm chewing Dentyne gum, so my breath should be bearable. He excuses himself to get us some punch. And that's when I hear the clock chime midnight. I know this sounds hockey, like a scene from a children's storybook, but seriously, I've got to make a run for it. Earlier, I'd promised myself I'd not stay past eleven o'clock since I have an early morning meeting. But somehow, time slipped away; now, it's midnight—the bewitching hour.

I'm torn between spending time with this intriguing guy or getting adequate rest before tomorrow's crucial meeting with a potential client. This meeting is so important that I'm meeting with a client on a Sunday. He wants to seal the deal with my firm before leaving town to meet with his partners. Losing this client's business is not an option. So, the need for sleep wins out, and I rush out of the building to go home.

Once home, I realize that my sterling silver initial pinkie

ring, which Kip gave me on our first anniversary, is missing from my finger. It's noticeable because I've never taken it off since Kip lovingly placed it on my finger. Where on earth could I have misplaced it? The last time I saw it was when the mysterious masked man at the ball took my hand and examined the ring. That was the last time I recall laying eyes on it. It must have slipped off at the ball.

Dayum, that ring represents everything that is truly precious to me in my relationship with Kip. It's my only physical reminder of the man I deeply love.

CHAPTER 4

Sunday morning, November 7
my condo

One of the things I love about weekend mornings is that I don't have Joshua or Dexter underfoot at the condo. They sleep in at their own place, allowing me to savor two peaceful and relaxing mornings all to myself. Don't get me wrong, I adore those boys more than anything, but seriously, can't I have one or two mornings off from them? A little *me-time*, you know?

Unfortunately, today is not that morning. I've got a nine o'clock meeting scheduled with a potential client to discuss financing for a massive residential subdivision project. Landing this client could put my firm on the map, attracting other developers seeking financing expertise. My future is riding on today's meeting—it has to go well.

As much as I'd love to be lazy and unwind, it's time to switch gears and get into a professional mindset. I must ace this meeting. The stakes are high, but the potential rewards are even greater.

Sitting alone at my breakfast nook, I'm mentally prepping for this upcoming meeting. I chug the last of my lukewarm coffee, feeling the caffeine kick in. Taking a deep breath, I mentally pump myself to pull myself together and get dressed. I rinse the empty coffee mug and flip it over in the sink. It's been a solid four months since Kip was taken away, but I still catch myself doing things as if he's still here—just like I did with the coffee mug. We always rinsed and set them upside down in the sink until later when one of us would place them in the dishwasher. Usually, that was Kip. He knew how much I pride myself on keeping a spic and span kitchen.

It's the little things that really get to me. You know? Like when I catch myself automatically setting a place for Kip at the supper table or not hogging the blanket at night. And sometimes, I even find myself making one of Kip's favorite meals. But then reality hits me: Kip isn't here anymore, and he won't be coming back—not for another forty-nine years and eight months. Man, that's an insanely long time to wait for someone, even when you love them.

CHAPTER 5

Same day, close to lunchtime
my condo

As the elevator doors swoosh open, I spot Joshua and Dexter sitting outside my condo door.

"Man," Joshua hops up from the floor, eyes wide, "where have you been?"

Before I can utter a word, Dexter springs to his feet.

"Seriously, Uncle Shane?" Dexter says. "You're just now getting home?"

"Chill, guys!" I throw my hands up in surrender. "I wasn't partying all night. Believe it or not, I had an early morning meeting with a client."

"But Uncle Shane," Joshua says, tilting his head and narrowing his eyes. "Today's Sunday. Your office is closed on the weekends."

"Yeah," I nod, sliding my key into the door lock. "But this was an important client. He was anxious to seal the deal before leaving town to meet with his partners. He's on a plane to California as we speak."

"So?" Dexter asks, raising an eyebrow. "Did you close the deal?"

"Yup," I grin. "Now you boys can relax; Kip and I can cover your rent for the rest of your lease." Kip and I have more than enough finances to handle their lease. I'm just messing with them, trying to crack a joke. Unfortunately, my attempt at humor falls flat.

"Hey, Uncle Shane," Dexter says. "We know you've been paying our rent."

"Yeah," Joshua chimes in. "Dad's stuck in the pen, so we know he's not writing checks."

I pause for a moment, considering their words.

"Well, guys," I say. "I think Kip wants you to believe he's still contributing. Plus, the money comes from Kip's and my joint bank account."

Without saying another word, I go inside.

Joshua and Dexter follow.

The atmosphere in the apartment is more relaxed, yet the tension in the air remains.

"Uncle Shane?" Dexter starts. "There's something that Josh and me have been thinking about..."

"Josh *and I*," I instantly correct without giving it a second thought.

"Okay, okay," Dexter grumbles, clearly annoyed. "Josh *and I*, we've been talking, and, well, we don't think it's right—"

"Yeah, since Dad is locked up for a long time..." Joshua jumps in, his voice filled with conviction.

"Josh *and I*—we—" Dexter interrupts, accentuating his grammar, wanting to get it correct.

"Alright, alright, guys," I say. "Let's sit down and have a chat."

Joshua and Dexter take seats on the couch.

"We agree that it's time for you to start dating again," Joshua says. "You shouldn't have to be alone just because of my dad. Well, you know what we mean?"

"This is unexpected," I say, sitting in the occasional chair adjacent to the couch. "Where's this coming from?"

"I... I mean," Joshua stammers. "Dex and I want you to know that we won't freak out if you start dating."

"But, Josh," I protest. "What about your dad? He and I are in a committed relationship."

"Well," Joshua explains, "the situation changed when Dad got himself locked up. Don't you think? It's not much of a relationship when you're here, and he's three hundred miles away in a prison cell."

"Hey, Uncle Shane," Dexter pipes up, "Josh and I don't think you should be alone forever. You know?"

"Wait a sec, Josh," I jump in, "what about your dad?"

"Well, considering everything," Joshua shrugs, "I think he'd be on board with Dex and me. It's not like the two of you were married or anything."

Let me tell you, those boys gave me a lot to think about. Am I truly prepared to dive back into the dating scene? Kip and I are in a rather delicate situation. It's not as if he's passed away or we've had a horrendous breakup. He's still alive and is a three-hour drive away. However, the miles and Plexiglas visitor window between us make it seem like we live in entirely different worlds.

Maybe the boys are onto something. Waiting for someone for fifty years is a long time, especially when there's no guarantee that we will have the same feelings for each other when he gets out.

After a few moments of consideration, I momentarily hit the pause button on this dating talk. The boys are starving, and honestly, so am I. Plus, after landing today's business deal, calls for a celebratory lunch. I just closed the largest deal of my career and am ready to celebrate. So, why not treat the boys and myself to brunch? I don't feel much like cooking or making a mess in the kitchen. Let someone else do the cooking and cleaning. Do you catch my drift?

Dale Thele

CHAPTER 6

Wednesday evening, November 10
my condo

I'm cleaning the kitchen after serving Joshua, Dexter, and myself supper. Let me tell you, those boys practically live here. They're here more often than at their costly apartment that I'm paying for. If I had more than one guest bedroom, I'd totally move them in here. Of course, there'd go what little privacy I have. Don't get me wrong; I enjoy their company. Especially since Kip got arrested, they're probably worried I'll feel lonely. It's sweet, but I appreciate a little privacy since they have their own apartment. You know, maybe I'd like to strip down and dance about the condo naked as a jaybird—you know? Or perhaps pop a naughty VHS porn into the trusty ol' VCR. But that's out of the question when Joshua and Dexter are almost always here. And I'm not one of those kinky uncles from the porn videos that get it on with his nephews. Yew! Watching and doing it in real life is a whole other story.

Maybe I'm getting greedy and want additional me-time and my few precious hours on Saturdays and Sundays. Do you know what I'm saying?

The boys are supposedly doing their homework in the living room. I have a sneaky suspicion they're watching TV instead.

"Hey, are you guys working on your homework?" I call out from the kitchen, attempting to hide any hint of suspicion.

"Of course, Uncle Shane!" Dexter yells back, followed by a chorus of giggles.

Suddenly, the TV volume drops so low that I can barely make out the sound.

I chuckle to myself and shake my head in amusement.

Just then, the doorbell rings.

"I got it!" Joshua shouts excitedly.

After wiping the kitchen counter, I drape the damp tea towel on the countertop to dry. Curious, I go to the living room to see who's at the door.

"Uncle Shane," Joshua says to me, his face skewed into an odd expression. "This guy claims he found your ring?"

"Oh, really?" I reply with a wary smile, moving to the open door.

"I believe we spoke on the phone earlier?" the man says.

"I'm Shane Davison," I introduce myself, extending my hand for a handshake.

"Kelly Johnson," he says, shaking my hand. "I found your lost ring." He reaches inside the pocket of his windbreaker jacket and produces a silver-toned ring. He holds it up for me to see it.

"May I?" I ask, seeking permission before taking the ring from his fingers.

The man nods, granting permission.

I examine the ring closely. My excitement quickly fades.

"I'm sorry, but this isn't my ring," I say, shaking my head.

"But the newspaper ad said *a silver ring with an engraved cursive letter D*," the man insists. "This ring is silver and has a fancy D engraving."

"You're right," I acknowledge. "However, the ring I'm looking for is made of sterling silver, while this one appears to be stainless steel."

"I'm certain it's sterling," the man insists.

"Sorry, I'm afraid it's not," I say. "Sterling silver is stamped with the number *925* or the word *sterling*. Unfortunately, the stamp on this ring reads *Made in China*. I'm sorry." With that, I place the ring in the man's palm. "I thank you for your time."

The man harrumphs, clearly annoyed. He spins on his heels to storm down the hall toward the elevator.

I chuckle to myself as I shut the door.

"Uncle Shane," Joshua inquires, "what was that about?"

"Well," I sigh, "I suppose you boys are bound to find out

sooner or later."

"Find out what?" Joshua asks.

"Josh, I misplaced the initial pinkie ring your dad gave me. It's been eating at me ever since I realized it was gone."

"Do you have any idea where you might have lost it?" Dexter asks.

"I have a hunch that I lost it at the Policeman's Ball," I confess.

"But you said you weren't going," Joshua points out.

"How did you put it?" Dexter mimics me. *"It's a shindig for couples, and since Kip can't go, I'm nothing more than the other half of a couple."*

"Dexter," I tease, "are you a parrot?"

"I just repeated what *you* said," Dexter defends himself.

"The one time you actually pay attention to what I say, and you use it against me," I grin.

"Well, what can I say?" Dexter shrugs.

"Is it a crime for me to change my mind and have gone to the ball?" I ask. "Now I regret going. If I'd stayed home, I'd still have my ring."

"Are you certain you lost it at the ball?" Dexter probes.

"I realized it was missing after I returned home," I explain. "Honestly, I'm not sure when or where I lost it."

"When was the last time you saw the ring?" Joshua asks.

"At the ball," I say. "I was talking to this guy. He commented on it. I held out my hand so he could get a better look at it."

"There you have your answer. I bet that guy swiped it right off your finger," Dexter remarks confidently. "Those types are sneaky. They'll snatch anything they can get their hands on."

"I highly doubt he was a thief," I counter.

"You can never be too sure about strangers," Dexter insists.

"I assure you, he didn't steal my ring," I say.

"How can you be so certain?" Dexter probes.

"Trust me," I say. "He was a nice, decent man."

"What was his name?" Dexter inquires.

"Well, um," I stumble. "Now that I think about it, we didn't exchange names. Okay, enough of this. We know I had it at the ball, but it was gone when I got home."

"Did you call the venue?" Joshua suggests. "They probably find all sorts of things after an event."

"Yep," I nod. "I called the venue, the catering company, even the police auxiliary. No one had information about a found ring."

"What about that eccentric Johnson guy who was just here?" Dexter asks. "What did he mean when he referred to a notice in the newspaper?"

"I placed an ad in the newspaper," I explain. "I'm offering a reward for the return of the ring, no questions asked."

"Oh, crap," Dexter exclaims, shaking his head. "Do you realize you opened Pandora's box? Every nut job in town will be calling to claim the reward."

"Honestly," I sigh. "I hadn't thought this through. All I want is my ring back."

CHAPTER 7

Saturday evening, November 13
my condo

The boys are seated at the supper table like they do most evenings. However, this evening, their behavior is peculiar. They squirm in their chairs, restless as if sitting on a mound of angry fire ants.

Curios, I address the elephant in the room.

"Alright," I say, my tone laced with intrigue. "I sense that something's up. And it's definitely not my imagination."

"What on earth are you talking about?" Dexter feigns innocence with a mischievous glint in his eyes.

"Oh, please!" I chuckle, not falling for his act. "I wasn't born yesterday. Come now, tell me, what are you boys up to?"

Joshua clears his throat and takes a deep breath.

"Alright," Joshua says, "remember when that Johnson guy came here earlier this week to return your ring?"

"Yes," I nod, "the ring that wasn't mine. Go on."

"Have you been getting many calls from that newspaper ad you placed?" Joshua asks.

"Yeah, there've been a few," I reply. "But the ring is still nowhere to be found. What's with all the sudden interest in my ring?"

"Well, it's not so much about your ring," Dexter says. "It's more about how you're going about trying to find it."

"Yeah, I get it," I admit, shaking my head. "I messed up by offering a reward—"

"No, that's not it," Dexter interrupts. "It's something else."

"It's about the notice you put in the newspaper," Joshua says.

"What about the notice?" I ask.

"Well, that notice gave Dex and me an idea," Joshua says.

29

"What kind of idea?" I inquire. "Should I be concerned?"

"Oh, no," Joshua shakes his head. "It's nothing bad."

"But?" I press. "Why do I have a feeling you guys are up to something? Come on, what are you not telling me?"

"We kind of placed a personals ad in the newspaper," Joshua admits.

"That's all?" I question. "So, which of you boy's placed an ad?"

The boys exchange curious glances before gasping for air, like fish out of water.

"Wel-l-l..." Joshua stammers. "We placed it for you."

"For me?" I exclaim. "Why on earth would you do something like that?"

"We saw how the notice you posted about your lost ring was getting responses," Dexter explains. "So, we thought a personals ad might have the same effect if we submitted one for you."

"We knew you wouldn't do something like that for yourself," Joshua adds. "So, we took the liberty of doing it for you."

"Seriously?" I shake my head in disbelief. "Please, tell me you're messing with me, and you didn't actually do it."

"Alright," Dexter says, "we didn't do it. But that doesn't change the fact that we did."

"Bonehead," Joshua exclaims, giving Dexter a smack up the side of the head.

"Ouch," Dexter winces, massaging his head. "What was that for?"

"For being a nitwit," Joshua retorts. "Sometimes your ideas are just downright absurd."

"Hey, hold on," I interject. "Name-calling won't solve anything here. Plus, the damage has already been done."

"What damage?" Dexter asks, clearly confused.

"The ad," Joshua says to Dexter. "We've already placed it. There's nothing we can do to fix things now."

"What's going on with you, Dex?" I inquire. "You're acting as if you've recently had a lobotomy."

"It's nothing, Uncle Shane," Joshua interjects. "He's just a bit out of it because he hasn't slept for a few nights."

"Are you having trouble sleeping?" I probe.

"Nah, it's not that," Joshua explains. "He's got a killer exam coming up, so he's been pulling all-nighters studying."

"Dex," I say with sincere concern, "you can't keep up that pace. You're going to burn out."

"It's no use, Uncle Shane," Joshua says. "I keep telling him that, but he won't listen. He's hooked on coffee and caffeine pills."

"Dex," I continue, "you really need to take better care of yourself."

"I know," Dexter admits. Then, with a hint of confusion, he adds, "Wait, Uncle Shane, how did we go from talking about you to talking about me?"

"Alright, you caught me," I confess with a mischievous grin. "I intentionally changed the subject without being obvious."

"Well," Joshua interjects, "no matter what you think about the ad we placed, it doesn't change the fact that you've already received a couple of replies."

"How cool is that?" Dexter adds.

The boys have no idea. I've tried the personals ad route before, but it didn't turn out so hot. It was several years back when, out of nowhere, this guy named Michael responded to my ad. And let me tell you, my life changed from that point on. The two months I spent with him were indescribable until—out of the blue—he suddenly kicked the bucket, and on my birthday, no less. After that experience, I'm not convinced that personals ads are the best way to meet guys for dating. Do you catch my drift?

CHAPTER 8

Monday evening, November 15
my condo

Joshua and Dexter have been tight-lipped about the guys who supposedly replied to the personals ad they posted on my behalf. I doubt there have been as many responses as they'd like me to believe. However, there's at least one since I'm about to go on my first blind date arranged by the boys. Joshua and Dexter take care of the replies, arrange the details of the dates, make the reservations, etc. All I have to do is go where they tell me to go. The rest is up to me. Can you believe they actually consider themselves matchmakers? Well, after tonight's date, I'll be the judge of their matchmaking abilities.

"Come on, Uncle Shane!" Joshua shouts from the living room. "Aren't you ready yet?"

"Hey, cut me some slack," I reply, entering the living room from the bedroom while adjusting my belt. "It's been ages since I've been on a date. Give me a break, will you?"

"Uncle Shane? Really?" Dexter says. "That belt with those shoes? Seriously? Don't you know that shoes and belts are to always, always, always match? Wasn't that spelled out in the *Welcome To Being A Homosexual Handbook?*" Dexter grins mischievously.

"The belt is fine," Joshua adds.

"Come on, Josh, really? You have no sense of fashion," Dexter shakes his head teasingly. "Straight guys like you don't have fashion sense."

"Hey," Joshua retorts. "If it was a big deal, I'd've said something. It's just a belt, man. Chill out."

"Uncle Shane needs to make a good impression," Dexter

fusses, his voice filled with concern. "As the old saying goes, *first impressions are everything*."

I pause for a moment, contemplating his words.

"You know what? Maybe I should change this belt," I suggest, turning towards the bedroom.

"Uncle Shane, you look fine," my ever-supportive nephew, Joshua, interjects.

"Fine?" I repeat, with frustration in my voice. "Fine, he says," I exclaim, throwing my arms up. "Nope, I can't do this."

"You can't back out now," Dexter says. "Everything's all set up. Put yourself in your date's shoes. How would you feel if you were stood up?"

I briefly consider the question.

"Right now? I'd be relieved to be stood up," I respond with a hint of sarcasm.

"No, you wouldn't," Dexter retorts, dismissing my concerns. "It's just a case of nerves."

Frustrated, I continue to pace the living room, questioning my sanity.

"I can't believe I let you boys talk me into this. Seriously, I need my head examined."

"Take a deep breath," Dexter says, trying to calm me. "Inhale. Hold. Now, exhale slowly."

Unfortunately, his advice only triggers a coughing fit.

"Quick, get Uncle Shane some water!" a panicking Joshua urges Dexter.

Dexter disappears into the kitchen. Before I can comprehend what's happening, he's shoving a glass of water in my face.

"Here," Dexter says, offering the glass. "Drink this. You'll feel better."

Expectantly, I take a sip of the water, but to my disappointment, I don't feel any different. Well, maybe I could drain my bladder, but I'd gone earlier; that's all I think at the moment. Resuming my nervous pacing, I can't shake my uneasy nerves.

"Uncle Shane, maybe you're approaching the situation all

wrong," Joshua suggests. "Instead of considering it a date, imagine having dinner with an old friend you haven't seen in a long time."

"I'm not meeting a friend," I object. "I'm meeting a complete stranger. Someone I know nothing about. There's no way I can do this."

"Yes, you can," Dexter assures while adjusting my shirt collar.

"Alright, fine. Instead of an old friend," Dexter proposes. "Pretend he's a potential new client, and you're meeting this guy for the first time because you want his business."

"Okay, that's something I can do," I concede. "But what if, after dinner, he wants to get down to business?"

"It's not like you're inexperienced," Joshua remarks. "You know what to do."

"Hold on a second," I interject. "I agreed to go on a date. Not a casual hookup."

"Whatever you decide is entirely up to you," Dexter says with a smug wink.

"Dex, will you stop," Joshua says. "You're not helping."

I nervously wring my hands, feeling the mounting pressure.

"Alright, Uncle Shane," Joshua says firmly. "Enough stalling. It's time for you to go, or you'll be really late."

"But," I try stalling. "Being fashionably late is a trademark for us gays."

"You'll be fashionably late enough to make a grand entrance, that's for sure," Dexter adds, pushing me towards the door. "Now, get out of here!"

"Fine, fine, I'm going," I say. "There's no need to be pushy."

I pause for a moment, then turn to face Dexter.

He adjusts my sports coat collar for the millionth time.

"Do I look alright?" I ask. "Be honest."

"You look absolutely fantastic," Dexter assures me, nudging me out the door of my own condo. "Now go."

With that, Dexter slams the door shut and bolts the lock.

That's how my evening starts, with Joshua and Dexter sending me on my first date since Kip. I'm feeling strange and fear my nerves will get the better of me. It's a lot like when Momma walked me to school on my first day of grade school. She held my hand and walked next to me. I think I jabbered nonsense all the way. Not that the three city blocks were all that far. Once we got to the school, Momma nudged me toward the door. It was scary, knowing that when I let loose of her hand, I'd be on my own. But you know something, I survived. Now, as an adult, it's time I buck up, face my fears, and meet my blind date.

The restaurant where I'm meeting my mystery date is just a few blocks from my condo. I've been here countless times with Kip, but this is my first time solo.

"Good evening, Monsieur Davison," the maitre d' welcomes me as I enter the restaurant. "Will Monsieur Benson be joining you?"

Talk about an awkward moment. Apparently, the maitre d' didn't get the memo that Kip won't be coming—not for a very long time.

"No. Mr. Benson and I are no longer together," I say, sensing a lump forming in my throat. It's one of the most challenging things I've had to say aloud. Kip's friends and mine know the situation, so there's been little discussion about it—until now.

"I'm very sorry to hear that, Monsieur Davison," the maitre d' sympathizes. "You and Monsieur Benson made a handsome couple."

"Thank you, Jacques," I reply, my voice filled with gratitude. "You've always been very kind to us."

"Je vous remercie for your gracious words, Monsieur Davison," the maitre d' responds.

"This is embarrassing," I tell the maitre d'. "I'm meeting someone, but we've not met before this evening."

"Oui, Monsieur," the maitre d' responds. "Your dinner companion is already here. Follow me, s'il vous plaît."

I trail behind Jacques, the maitre d', as he leads me to a table where a man sits, his back towards me.

The maitre d' pulls out the chair for me.

I settle into the chair, sitting across the table from my mystery date.

My dinner companion lowers his wine glass.

"I hope you don't mind," he says. "I took the liberty of ordering for the both of us."

"No problem," I reply, sampling the wine and checking out my handsome date.

Unlike Kip, I'm no wine expert. He could sniff and taste a wine and tell you everything about its origin and contents. He effortlessly paired food and wine like me, ordering a cheeseburger, fries, and a coke. As for me and wine, I need to learn about wine pairing, so don't rely on me to do that. Kip had a refined palate, while I can't tell the difference between red and white unless I can see their colors. That's the extent of my wine knowledge, although I won't turn down a glass of wine with a meal.

As my mystery date studies the menu, I set my stemmed glass on the table, taking advantage of the moment to get a gander at him. He's about my height and age. His wavy black hair and deep brown eyes—almost black—catch my attention. I'm a little envious of his thick, neatly trimmed mustache and beard. Unlike him, I struggle to grow decent facial hair, so I settle for a daily shaving routine.

But what really strikes me is his incredible smile. It's hard to put into words, except that it's perfect. Observing him, I assume he's probably a mix of Hispanic and white. His complexion is on the lighter side, which makes me think he can't be entirely Hispanic.

Overall, I can't deny the intrigue that surrounds my mystery man. His appearance, with the combination of attractive features and that captivating smile, makes me want to know more about him.

Extending his hand across the table, he introduces himself.

"The name's Griffin, but everyone calls me Griff," he says.

"Pleasure to meet you, Griff. I'm Shane," I reply, feeling a rush of heat surging up the back of my neck. The boys had already given Griff my name, so why did I reintroduce myself? I'm so-o-o embarrassed. My cheeks burn hot, and I wish I could disappear beneath the table. I can't believe I've already made a fool of myself in a matter of minutes. Griff must think I'm a complete idiot.

To my surprise, Griff flashes a warm smile.

"You're cute," he says, causing my face to flush even more. Attempting to hide my embarrassment, I grab my goblet and sip my wine, using the goblet to hide my blushing face. Peeking out from behind the glass, I can't shake the feeling that there's something familiar about Griff. I can't put my finger on it. I'm sure we've met before. I dismiss the thought, hoping I'll recall where we previously met during our meal.

CHAPTER 9

First date

I remember going on my first actual date when I was in the second or third grade. Calling it a *date* is a stretch. It was more like two elementary school friends going together to a Saturday afternoon matinée magic show.

Momma fretted about her preparations for the big event getting ruined if there was rain. It was an overcast day, and she was worried sick. To make matters worse, she made me take a morning bath. Now, let me tell you, I never took morning baths. Our family always bathed in the evenings. But, on this day, Momma insisted I take a morning bath before the matinée show.

When I got home from school the day before the show, Momma took me to the barbershop for a haircut. I couldn't understand why she was so insistent, considering I was due to get my ears lowered in just one week. Momma had this thing where she'd drag me to the barber every two weeks, whether I needed it or not. Going a week early messed up the whole hair-cutting schedule.

I couldn't help but ask, *Will I have to get another haircut next week to get everything back on track?*

Seriously, why get a haircut one week early? It didn't make sense to me.

Shut it, Momma told me, *mind your business, and do as I say.*

I thought I *was* minding my business by asking about getting my hair cut a week early. But apparently, I was wrong. Confusion overwhelmed me, preventing me from asking further questions, so I shut my trap. I figured I'd better understand when I was an adult. I'm an adult now, and I still don't comprehend some things Momma said and did.

Momma washed and pressed my Sunday church shirt, making me polish and shine my leather dress shoes. Was all this extra effort necessary for a Saturday afternoon kid's magic show? And to make matters worse, Momma told me not to get my clothes dirty at the show because I'd have to wear the same clothes to church the next day. She mentioned there wouldn't be time to wash and press my shirt again when I returned from the matinée. Can you believe that?

All this hoopla because of a magic show for kids. I couldn't understand why I had to dress up like I was going to church. And to make matters worse, Momma wouldn't let me go to the show alone. She made me ask Diane Erwin, a girl-type friend from school. Her daddy worked with my daddy at the Post Office. Sometimes, Mr. and Mrs. Erwin came to our house, and the grown-ups played card games in the kitchen while Diane and I played outside in the backyard. Why the backyard? We could play in three places, but Momma said it wasn't proper for a boy to take a girl to his bedroom. So, that left two places we were allowed to go: the living room or the backyard. If we played in the living room, we'd get yelled at for making noise. So, the backyard was where we played.

Diane introduced me to this cool game called *Moon Man*. It was the perfect activity for those late evenings when the three Erwin's came to our house, and the moon was shining bright. Let me break the game down for you: Diane and I would go on a scavenger hunt in my backyard, searching for scraps of paper that had blown into the yard. Once we found one, one of us would read the imaginary message on the paper, pretending they were written by the man who lived on the moon. Of course, we made up the messages to give each other a good scare. Our favorite theme was always Martians invading Earth. When we ran out of scrap papers, we switched to fallen leaves from the trees in my yard. We'd play the game until the adults grew tired of their card games. Then, Diane and her parents went home.

Little did I know, Momma, Daddy, Mr. and Mrs. Erwin conspired to set me up on a matinée date with Diane.

Unfortunately, I caught wind of their plan a little too late. Truth be told, I wasn't interested in Diane in a romantic sense. She was a friend, a pal, someone I played *Moon Man* with, and that was the extent of our relationship. At nine or ten years of age, I was far too engrossed in my pet turtle and stamp collecting to be bothered with girls. At the time, I didn't yet know that in a few years, I would blossom into a flaming homosexual.

On the day of the magic show, I was excited because I absolutely loved magicians. I was given a magic kit for Christmas a couple of years before, and ever since I'd learned of the matinée, I'd been honing my magic skills. I was excited to be going to a real magic show.

After lunch, Daddy drove me to the Erwin's house to pick up Diane. When we pulled into their driveway, I was ready to leap from the car to get her.

But my daddy interrupted my eagerness, saying, *Hold on, son.*

I vividly recall that moment when I abruptly shot him a puzzled look. The clock was ticking, and I had to rush to get Diane, fearing we might miss the show's start.

To my surprise, Daddy reached into the back seat and produced a small bouquet of flowers.

"What are these for?" I asked.

"Give them to Diane," he said.

"But why?" I questioned.

"It's a friendly gesture," Daddy explained.

"But what if she doesn't want flowers?" I persisted.

"Trust me," Daddy assured me. "She will."

Shrugging, I took the flowers in my grubby little hand, then excitedly leaped out of the car and rushed to the front door. I pressed the doorbell. Impatiently, I waited for an answer so I could give the flowers to Diane. We had to get going so we wouldn't be late for the show's start. There was no time to waste.

Mrs. Erwin opened the door, "Hello, sir. How may I help

you?"

"It's me, Shane Davison. Don't you know me?" I said.

"Oh my goodness," she exclaimed, taken aback. "I didn't recognize you. You look so dashing and mature in that suit."

I must have blushed because my face and neck suddenly felt hot. Damnit!

"Is Diane ready to go?" I asked, tugging at my starched shirt collar, which was strangling me.

"I'm ready," Diane announced, brushing past her mother.

Diane looked beautiful in her frilly dress, rustling petticoat, lace-topped anklets, and shiny black patent leather Mary Jane shoes.

"Here," I said, pushing the flowers at her. "These are for you. My daddy said it's something nice I'm supposed to do."

Diane took the flowers and buried her nose in them.

"Thanks," she said.

"Let me put those in water," Mrs. Erwin offered, taking the bouquet from Diane. "You two should scoot so you aren't late."

I don't know why, but I grabbed Diane's hand, and we skipped hand in hand to the car. I suppose I did that to speed things up and get to the theater on time.

Daddy didn't park the car when he pulled up to the theater because all the parking spaces were full. Instead, he stopped in the street, causing the drivers behind us to honk their horns. He let us out of the car and then drove away.

Diane and I went inside to spend the money Momma gave me for tickets, popcorn and cokes for the both of us.

I found myself at a loss as we entered the dimly lit theater. I had been there once before with my aunt, uncle, and cousins to watch the movie *Pinocchio*. Back then, my uncle led us in and out of the dark theater. But this time, I was on my own, with no one to guide me. So, I threw caution to the wind and figured things out as I went along.

Some of Diane's friends sat up front by the stage, enthusiastically waving for us to join them. Although I didn't know the names of the girls and boys, they appeared to be friendly enough. Diane and I happily took the two seats they had saved.

When the lights went down and the curtains opened, I clapped my hands like a madman. At that moment, I completely lost track of everything and everyone around me. I found myself at a mesmerizing magic show, where nothing could break my concentration as the magician wowed the audience with his mind-boggling tricks. First, he pulled a live rabbit out of a hat, leaving me in awe. Then, he poured milk into a newspaper funnel; to this day, I have no clue where that milk went. As if that wasn't enough, he pulled a long string of multi-colored scarves from his empty hand. But then things got really weird.

The magician asked for a volunteer from the audience. Without hesitation, my arm shot up like a rocket. And guess what? He picked me. Me, of all people. I raced up the stairs to the stage, eager to stand beside my newfound idol. The excitement was so overwhelming that I don't recall what happened next. All I remember is the thunderous applause from the audience and the magician thanking me for my assistance. I stumbled back to my seat, dazed by the fact that I'd played a part in the magician's act, even though I didn't remember anything I'd done on that stage. To be perfectly honest, I'm pretty sure he put me in a trance of some sort.

After the show, Diane and I went outside the theater. It was raining, so we huddled under the awning to avoid getting wet. I looked and looked, but I couldn't see Daddy's car anywhere. Cars were everywhere, picking up kids who'd been to the show. Some of the cars had their headlights on. Others were honking their horns. On top of that, it was raining cats and dogs. It was a madhouse, and I still couldn't see my daddy's car.

Suddenly, a boy who'd sat in the front row approached Diane and whispered something in her ear.

She flashed him a smile, said *so long* to me, and then strolled off with that boy.

He had an umbrella.

Meanwhile, I was stranded under the theater awning, patiently waiting for my daddy to arrive since I didn't have an umbrella.

Waiting under the awning, I'm unsure what I felt when Diane left with that boy. It was like feeling sad and mad at the same time. Maybe it was a mix of sadness and anger that she picked him over me. I mean, I didn't have romantic feelings for her. I thought of her as a friend from school. But still, there was this strange emotion bubbling up inside me that I couldn't put my finger on. It was unfamiliar; I didn't like or understand it because I was just a kid standing under an awning, trying to keep from wetting rained on.

CHAPTER 10

Tuesday morning, November 16
my condo

The doorbell rings.

I know who it is. What I don't understand is why they don't just walk in? It's not like I lock the door or anything. Lately, it seems Joshua and Dexter are spending more time here than at their apartment. I enjoy their company, but why are they always here?

I twist the door nob and swing open the door.

Dexter pushes his way ahead of Joshua, past me, heading for the kitchen.

"What's for breakfast?" Dexter asks, sniffing the air.

"I'm so hungry I can eat anything that doesn't run away from me," Joshua announces, following close behind.

I find myself holding the door open for absolutely no one. Shaking my head in resignation, I close the door to move through the living room, heading for the kitchen.

"Hey, Uncle Shane, where are the pancakes?" Dexter says, searching the kitchen.

"Sorry, no pancakes this morning," I say.

"Darn," Dexter mutters, clearly disappointed. "I was looking forward to some of your buttermilk pancakes."

"Well, why don't you put in your order today for tomorrow's breakfast?" Joshua says.

"That's not a bad idea," Dexter says, his face lighting up. "Uncle Shane, consider this my official pancake order for tomorrow morning."

"Same here," Joshua adds.

"See?" Dexter exclaims. "Even Josh is craving pancakes."

I can't help but smile and shake my head.

"Uncle Shane?" Joshua asks as he fills two mugs of coffee, one for himself and one for Dexter. "How did your date go last night?"

"That's right," Dexter says, accepting a mug of coffee from Joshua. "Did you get lucky?"

"Dex, you never cease to amaze me," I chuckle.

Joshua nudges Dexter in the ribs.

"What's that for?" Dexter protests.

"Dex, Uncle Shane went on a date," Joshua informs Dexter. "It wasn't a hookup."

"Yeah, I know that," Dexter responds. "It's just that sometimes..."

"Hold on a second," I quickly interject before Dexter can finish his thought. "Let's not go down that road."

"So, how did the date go?" Joshua asks while taking a seat at the breakfast nook.

"Eh," I shrug and reply, "it was alright."

"Alright?" Dexter says. "Can you give us a little more than that?"

"I mean, it was just okay," I say. "Nothing extraordinary."

"Okay?" Joshua cuts in. "Is that a good kind of okay? Meaning you'll be going out again? Or was it just okay, meaning no, I'm not wasting my time?"

"I doubt I'll see him again," I say.

"What was wrong with him?" Dexter asks.

"Nothing," I reply. "I actually had a good time."

"Then why won't you see him again?" Dexter persists.

"We just didn't click, you know what I mean?" I say.

"But you said you had a good time..." a puzzled Dexter says.

"Well," I clarify, "people can enjoy each other's company without necessarily feeling a romantic connection."

There's more to the story, but I'd rather not talk about it. It's not that the date was terrible—honestly, it wasn't bad. It has more to do with what happened after the date that guaranteed there'd be no follow-up date. Even though he asked for my number. What the boys don't know won't hurt them. You know?

"Oh, I think I get it," Dexter says, pouring sugar into his coffee.

"Well, Uncle Shane," Joshua says. "Don't worry, as they say; *there are plenty more fish in the sea.*"

"Mm-hmm," Dexter says, stirring his coffee. "We've got more guys lined up for you."

Oh great, I'm thrilled. More chances to embarrass myself even further, I think to myself.

Dale Thele

CHAPTER 11

Wednesday evening, November 17
Chez Pierre Ristorante

Jacques, the elegant and polished maitre d', approaches as I enter the restaurant.

"How is Monsieur Davison this evening?" he asks with a charming smile.

"I'm doing well, Jacques," I reply.

"Your table is ready," he gestures for me to follow him. "This way, s'il vous plaît."

I sit across the table from a young man who definitely has my attention—and not in a good way. His jet-black hair is messy, and he sports dark makeup around his eyes and lips, contrasting with his ashen complexion. Dressed entirely in black, from his tee shirt, vintage suit jacket, black slacks, and shoes, he gives off a mysterious vibe.

Is he a teenage vampire? I think to myself.

Politely, my supper date rises halfway from his chair and extends his pale hand towards me.

"My name's Abacus," he introduces himself.

I'm figuring out the rationale behind the young man's peculiar presence. His parents practically ensured his transformation into a vampire by naming him ABACUS. How heartless of them. *Should I report the parents to Child Protective Services?*

I forgo shaking the pale hand, fearing he might mistake my wrist for a delectable appetizer. After all, we're not finalizing a deal that necessitates a firm, robust handshake.

"I'm Shane," I say. "Nice to meet you."

Nice? Nice, is that what I said? What can I say that conveys what I mean without coming off rude? I'm not pleased, honored, or happy to meet this—whatever he is. What on earth am I supposed to say next in this situation? How long have you been undead? Nervously, I readjust in my chair across from my vampire date, pondering what one discusses with a vampire. Interests? Hobbies? Blood types?

To put it mildly—and trust me, the less said, the better—the date was a total bust. We were like two jigsaw puzzle pieces—each from a different puzzle.

For example, when our food arrived, who would've thought a vampire could be a vegetarian? And how he meticulously picked at his salad, removing every last bit of dressing, was just too bizarre. It was like watching a deranged lab assistant dissect a lettuce leaf. Needless to say, it wasn't the most exciting or enjoyable date I've been on.

Something else that struck me as odd was that he drank tap water. I assumed he was underage to consume wine or other alcoholic beverages. That raised a concern for me—I've no desire to pursue an underage minor—or, in this case, an underage vampire. Surprisingly, he declined the bottled water, stating *it contained harmful chemicals*. I suppose vampires can drink regular tap water if it hasn't been blessed.

Overall, Abacus turned out to be a cheap date. Given our lack of shared interests, the evening ended once I polished off my delectable poulet roti and garlic-stuffed mushrooms, perfectly complemented by a refreshing Chenin Blanc. I must admit, I was afraid to order a beef dish—you know—the blood. Why risk triggering a vampire? Who wants to take that kind of risk? Am I right? Also, the side of garlic-stuffed mushrooms was ordered on purpose. I took appropriate precautions. I suppose baked garlic is as effective as raw in warding off vampires?

The date ended early. I got home in time to catch the second half of an evening sitcom before the nightly news started. The whole experience left me feeling disheartened about the possibility of meeting someone compatible. I'd been on two dates, and neither led to a second. Maybe I should throw in the towel and accept that I'm not dating material, you know?

Welcome to my pity party.

CHAPTER 12

Junior High sock hop

When I was thirteen and in my first year of junior high, I experienced my first honest-to-goodness actual date. The girl I was going steady with was a year older than me and had a ton of dating experience, which made me self-conscious since I was a newbie to the dating game. I followed her lead because I didn't want to expose my lack of experience compared to her vast knowledge.

On a Monday morning at school, the principal announced an upcoming event called a *sock hop* over the school's public address system. The event was scheduled for Friday after classes in the school gymnasium. I suppose I should tell you the reason behind the name—sock hop. It's a dance where everyone removes their shoes and dances in their socked feet to protect the polished wood gymnasium floor. While the *sock* part made sense, I've no idea where the *hop* comes into play.

My girlfriend's name was Morgan Duffy, and she was really eager to go to the sock hop. I would've been equally excited if I'd known how to dance.

At home, I moped around the house, feeling down because I didn't know how to dance.

Momma noticed my gloomy mood and asked what was bothering me.

I brushed it off, saying it was *nothing*.

However, as we all know, Mommas have a way of persisting until they get the answers they want.

"There's a school dance coming up," I told Momma.

Momma's eyes lit up like a Christmas tree.

"And?" she asked.

"Well," I mumbled, feeling embarrassed. "I don't know how to dance."

Momma burst into laughter.

It stung a little.

"Don't worry, sweetheart," she assured me. "I'll teach you how to dance."

Wow, do Mommas really know how to dance? I wondered.

Indeed, Momma was quite the dancer. She glided across the floor, gracefully moving to the rhythm of the old 78 RPM records on our phonograph player. She taught me what she referred to as *couple dancing*.

Initially, I was clumsy, often inadvertently stepping on her delicate toes. My footing was far from sure, and I was doubtful I'd be able to learn to dance. However, I gradually improved through sheer determination and lots of practice. Eventually, I reached a point where I could confidently dance with Momma, barely causing her any foot discomfort.

When Friday came, Morgan and I went to the gymnasium. We kicked off our shoes and went hand in hand onto the dance floor. I was ready to bust some moves, feeling confident and excited to dance. The music started, and I was taken aback. The kids weren't doing the kind of dancing Momma taught me. Instead of graceful moves, everyone was gyrating and twisting like crazy. I felt lost and confused. Standing there like a fool while everyone else was having a grand time. Frustration got the best of me, and I left the dance floor, finding solace on the bleachers, all by my lonesome.

I watched Morgan having a blast, dancing with various boys. Eventually, she left with a boy. It reminded me of when Diane left me for that other boy after we went together to the magic show matinée. All those emotions from that rainy afternoon resurfaced, leaving me feeling lost and uncertain.

I quietly slipped out of the gymnasium.

On my way home from the dance, I promised myself *I'd never go to another sock hop for as long as I lived. I'd never embarrass myself like that, ever again. Cross my heart and hope to die.*

Dale Thele

CHAPTER 13

Thursday morning, November 18
my condo

As the self-proclaimed chief cook and bottle washer of the unincorporated Davison diner, I'm frying bacon and flipping pancakes when the doorbell rings. With a quick wipe of my hands on a tea towel, I walk through the living room, still donning an apron. Though I'm dressed for work in a crisp white dress shirt, dark slacks, and polished leather oxfords, my shirt collar remains open at the neck, as I habitually put on my necktie when I leave for work. The apron protects against potential spills on my clothes. Yes, I'm accident-prone; I invariably splash something on myself no matter how careful I am.

Approaching the door, I casually toss the tea towel over my shoulder. No need to bother with the door peephole; I already know who is on the opposite side.

I swing the door open, and two overly rambunctious teenage boys rush inside.

"Morning, boys," I greet, but my words fall flat.

Joshua and Dexter hastily retreat to the kitchen as if they'd drawn free-out-of-jail cards from a Monopoly board game.

No pass go.
No collecting $200.
Follow the smell of cooking food.

Watching the boys nearly sprint to the kitchen, I wonder what would happen to them if I wasn't here to whip up their breakfasts and suppers. It's a bit concerning. You know? The only thing they can cook on their own is burnt water; in the process, they ruin the pot. They can't live on dried breakfast cereal alone. So, as an honorary uncle, what am I to do?

Let me give you some backstory on the boys so you can better understand the situation. Dexter's parents split up about a year ago; his dad moved to Tulsa shortly after the divorce. Then there's Cecily—Dexter's mom—who packed her shit and moved to Akron, Ohio, in June, transferring to another Dillingers Department Store. Poor Dexter was left without a parent nearby. And as for Joshua, well, his mom passed away while giving birth. He never got to know her. Cecily was the closest thing he had to a mom, but now she's gone too. And to top it all off, Joshua's dad is locked up in prison for a long, long time.

So that leaves me, honorary Uncle Shane, unexpectedly thrust into the role of adult guardian of two teenage boys. It's not a responsibility I take lightly, let me tell you. But hey, life sometimes throws a curve ball, right? Don't get me wrong, I love being an honorary uncle to these boys. However, I worry I might mess up and ruin their lives. I don't want them to end up bitter like my ol' man.

So yeah, it's a challenge, but I'm determined to do right by these boys. They deserve a stable and caring adult guardian; I want to be that person. Or rather, I want to fill that role the best I can.

"Do I smell my favorite? Buckwheat pancakes?" Dexter asks, a wide grin stretching across his face.

"But I thought buttermilk was your favorite?" I ask.

"That was yesterday," Dexter says. "Today's favorite is buckwheat 'cause that's what you're making."

I swear, that kid could survive solely on pancakes. It's all he ever wants for breakfast. Didn't Cecily ever make pancakes for him? Personally, I don't give in to all his cravings. I know he shouldn't have pancakes every morning. As a growing boy, he needs a balanced breakfast to start his day. I mix things up and make different breakfast options each morning. The same goes for supper. During weekdays, I can count on the boys to join me for breakfast and supper. For lunch, they purchase something to eat on campus. Dexter and Joshua each receive a hefty weekly allowance, so I don't worry about them missing lunch. I suppose you're wondering why two healthy and fit college boys are getting allowances. When Kip and I became a *couple,* we didn't want the boys to be distracted from their schoolwork by working part-time jobs. So, each boy receives the equivalent of the pay he'd get from working an afternoon and/or weekend job.

Following the boys to the kitchen, I pick up the boy's jackets and books they toss on the floor like a trail to the food. When I catch up with them, I see they've emptied the pot of coffee. Each has a mug in hand, making their way to the breakfast nook.

"So, how was your date last night?" Joshua asks me.

"Yeah, how did it go?" Dexter adds.

"What do you boys know about vampires?" I say.

"Why do you ask?" Joshua says. "Did something happen on your date?"

"Well, I think my date was a vampire," I say, forking crispy bacon slices from the hot skillet and placing them on a paper towel-covered platter.

"A vampire?" Dexter's eyes widen. "Seriously?"

"I think Uncle Shane's talking about a Goth," Joshua pipes in.

"Ew," Dexter responds, scrunching up his face as if he's just stepped in something soft and left by a large animal. "Those people dressed in all black? They give me the creeps."

"Tell me about it," I chime in. "The whole time, I swear to you, he was sizing me up like I was his next meal. Gave me the willies."

"Hey, Uncle Shane," Joshua says to me. "Goths aren't vampires. They're harmless pacifists."

"You can believe whatever you want, but you weren't sitting across from Abacus," I shoot back.

"*Abacus?*" Dexter says. "Like one of those old-timey counting things with the wires and beads?"

"Yup, Abacus," I confirm.

Dexter shakes his head, chuckling.

"I'm sorry I set you up with that guy," Joshua says, holding back a laugh. "If I'd known he was a total weirdo, I wouldn't've sent the two of you on a date."

"Don't sweat it," I assure Joshua. "Since you don't meet these guys in person, there was no way for you to know he was a complete whack-job."

"I'll try to better screen your future dates," Joshua says, stirring his coffee.

"Honestly, I think I'm done with dating," I say.

"What? Seriously?" Dexter asks, sounding surprised. "You've only been on two dates."

"Two dates too many," I reply, shaking my head.

"Hey, you can't give up now," Joshua insists, sounding all fired up. "You're just getting your feet wet."

"I feel like I'm drowning," I admit, feeling defeated.

"Come on, Uncle Shane," Joshua pleads. "Give us more time to find the perfect guy for you."

"I had the perfect guy," I say. "Kip checked all the boxes. You know?"

"But Dad's not around anymore," Joshua reminds me.

"Josh and I don't want to see you alone," Dexter adds.

"I'm not alone," I say. "I've got you boys."

"But we're not the same as someone—special," Joshua says, his voice trailing off.

"Go on a couple more dates, please?" Dexter pleads.

"Well—okay," I give in, against my better judgment. "I'll do it for you boys, but let's avoid more dates at Chez Pierre Ristorante. The staff there knows me—and they knew your dad."

"Got it," Joshua nods.

CHAPTER 14

Friday evening, November 19
Ted's Greek Taverna

This is my first time visiting this place. I've passed it countless times, yet I've never come inside for some unknown reason. However, tonight is different. I have a reason for being here. I'm meeting yet another blind date. I know nothing about this guy, but we'll meet through the supper reservation the boys made for us. This place gives off more of a diner vibe than a trendy restaurant. And judging by how packed it is, the food must be at least halfway decent.

I introduce myself to the hostess so she can direct me to my table.

She scans the names in the reservation book with her long, bony finger. As her perfectly manicured nail nears the end of the list, she shakes her head in disapproval.

"I don't see anything for *David and son*," she says, real snooty-like, which seems out of place for this modestly decorated restaurant.

"It's actually one word, *Davison*," I correct her, feeling increasingly irritated by this self-important hostess who thinks she's all that when, in reality, she's just a glorified door attendant with a bad attitude.

She rolls her eyes and lets out an exasperated sigh. Once again, her long, polished nail glides over the list of names. This time, it stops about one-third the way on the second page.

"Here you are," she says. "Sorry."

I immediately pick up on her one-word apology, which is as genuine as her fake nails. She snatches two menus and walks swiftly towards the dining area. I follow behind, anticipating being seated at a table near the restrooms or, even worse, in a stall inside the toilet. She's clearly annoyed with me. Not that I've done anything wrong—I simply corrected my name, which she misheard.

During the short stroll through the dining room, I evaluate the hostess. She has no business in that position, not with *that* sour disposition. Through the years, I've learned that people who are easily stressed and grumpy are unfit for customer service work. This hostess is definitely one of the unqualified.

The young woman gestures slightly to the only vacant table in the dining room. She slaps the menus on the table and storms off; her heavy-footed walk sounds like a clomping Clydesdale.

Diner's heads turn, shooting questioning looks at her.

Unconsciously, I release a sigh, relieved the annoying biatch is finally gone. With a self-conscious smile, I glance at the curious onlookers staring at me. Blushing, I sit at the table facing the door, strategically positioned to size up tonight's intended date before officially meeting.

An eager server steps up to the table. He appears to be a friendly young man, a college student, maybe. I wonder if he goes to the University of Texas. And if so, does he know Joshua or Dexter? But then again, UT is a huge school. The odds of this young man knowing my nephews are staggering.

"What can I get you to drink, sir?" the server asks, reminding me of a bartender in a gay bar.

Immediately, my gaydar goes off. Ding. Ding.

Both of us sense the undeniable gay vibe in the air.

He flashes a mischievous smile as if he's just stumbled upon his next sugar daddy.

I'm sensing his steamy gaze undressing me in a highly suggestive position on a vibrating motel bed. At the same time, sleazy straight porn blares on the TV, all before I can utter, "Bourbon and coke."

"Excellent, sir," he says suggestively, causing my body to react like I've taken a little blue pill.

Nervous, I gulp as he walks away, his slacks hugging his firm, taut buttocks.

Suddenly, I'm craving cake.

After two generously poured bourbon and cokes, I realize my date stood me up. The chair opposite me has remained vacant since arriving almost an hour ago. Feeling disheartened over a date that didn't happen, I've lost a large chunk of self-esteem and my appetite.

I request the check from the server.

As the server places the check on the table, he slips a piece of paper with what appears to be his name and phone number written on it. With a suggestive wink, he leaves me to consider his intentions.

If only I were younger, I think to myself.

I reach into my wallet. Pulling out a few bills, I place them on the drink check. The temptation to grab the slip of paper with the server's number is tempting, but I know deep down that he's too young. It would be like robbing the cradle, which I have no intention of getting involved. Besides, I'm raising two teenage boys already, so I don't need another.

Not wanting to stiff the kid, I add an extra twenty to the stack of bills, leaving the additional handwritten phone number untouched.

CHAPTER 15

Teenage crush

I remember when I was a junior in senior high school. I'd been openly gay for just over a year. However, I didn't have a boyfriend, mainly because there weren't any potential prospects since I was the only out gay student in the entire school. I longed for a boyfriend, but it seemed like fate had other plans.

Everything changed for me one June evening when this handsome man walked into the restaurant where I worked part-time as a dishwasher/busboy. I was nearly finished cleaning a table after a family of four had left when I noticed him enter the dining room. The hostess promptly seated him, and that's when our eyes met.

It was such a magical moment. When our eyes locked, a big smile lit up his face. I couldn't help but smile back at him, completely unable to resist. It felt like the lightning bolt of love hit us both at my after-school job.

As the evening progressed and he finished his meal, I strongly desired to approach him. But it wouldn't have been the proper thing to do. My boss would have given me a lecture on bothering a customer. *It's just not suitable for a busboy to interact with customers.* He'd say to me.

Regrettably, I watched the most attractive man I'd ever seen leave the restaurant and, with him, any chance of a real person-to-person connection.

I went to tidy up the table, and that's when I discovered a paper napkin with a message scribbled on it: *Call Me,* accompanied by a phone number and a name, *Kevin.*

Naturally, I was thrilled beyond words. I couldn't wait to dial the number and connect with him. However, I was at work, so I had to be patient. I'd phone him later when we could have a proper phone conversation. I was dying to hear his voice. It was all I could think about.

The following evening, I was off from my job at the restaurant, so I eagerly dialed Kevin's number from the napkin left last night.

A deep and melodious voice answered the phone, instantly making my heart flutter.

"Is this Kevin?" I asked, my heart racing with hope that it was the adorable guy I'd seen from the night before.

"Yes, this is Kevin," he hesitantly replied, confirming his identity.

I could hardly contain my excitement. It felt like I was about to burst with joy.

"This is Shane," I said. "I'm the busboy from the restaurant where you ate last night."

"Oh, okay," he hesitated. "Did *you* get my phone number?"

"Yes," I responded, feeling nervous and excited. "I found it while clearing your table."

"Um," he stammered, clearly flustered. "The note you found was intended for the waitress...not you."

"Oh," I said, trying to hide my disappointment. I was relieved he couldn't see the tears welling in my eyes or feel the lump forming in my throat.

There was an awkward silence on the phone.

"No worries, sir," I finally said, breaking the awkward tension. "I'll pass the note on to Brenda for you."

That was the most challenging thing I'd ever said to someone. I couldn't have done it if we were talking face-to-face, but I managed to say it over the phone.

"Thanks," he said.

There was another long, uncomfortable silence.

"I suppose I should let you go," I said, feeling an overwhelming desire to end the call.

"Yes," he replied.

"Goodbye," I finally managed to say.

"Bye," he said before abruptly hanging up.

I sat there, listening to the silence on the line. Perhaps I expected more from Kevin. Or maybe I was numb, still processing what had transpired. Either way, I listened to the air trapped in the telephone line for a very long while.

That was one of the rare moments when I broke a promise I'd made to someone. It felt exhilarating to embrace my rebellious side. Instead of delivering Kevin's note to Brenda, I took pleasure in tearing the napkin into tiny shreds and flushing it down the toilet, along with my dashed dreams and countless tears. Brenda will have lots of opportunities with guys, but I doubt I'll be so lucky.

Dale Thele

CHAPTER 16

Saturday evening, November 20
Ted's Greek Taverna

Strolling in from off the street into Ted's Greek Taverna, I'm greeted by a different hostess in contrast to the disaster of a hostess from last night. This young lady is polite and has a great personality. I would've hired her on the spot if I needed a receptionist. But honestly, I already have a really awesome guy. I couldn't manage without him—he's the best assistant ever. You're not interested in hearing about my assistant, so let's return to this new hostess. She's a vast improvement compared to the biatch from last night. Finding my name on the reservation list, she leads me to a different table from the previous evening. It's actually in a better location.

I sit at the table.

"Your server will be with you shortly," she says, giving me two menus. "Enjoy your meal." She smiles and returns to her front door post.

Out of the corner of my eye, I notice the server approaching, but I'm too nervous to look directly at him. What if it's the same server from last night? I'm definitely too young to be a sugar daddy. For clarification, at what age does someone become a bona fide sugar daddy? It's a question that's been bugging me since last night.

"Sir, would you care for a drink?" the server asks in a friendly manner.

Not recognizing the voice, I turn to face him. He's not the same server, instantly putting me at ease. A heavy sigh of relief escapes my lips.

The server raises an eyebrow, giving me a curious look.

"I'll have a bourbon and coke, please," I say. My voice

wavers as I'm not fully recovered from my apprehension that the server might have been the same as the previous night.

"Of course, sir," he replies before leaving.

I can't help but wonder what this new server must think of me. He probably sees me as some weirdo or something. But hey, why should I care about his opinion? He's not the one I'm trying to impress tonight. That's reserved for my date, assuming this one shows up. A sense of unease creeps in as I glance at the empty chair across from me. Will I get stood up for the second night in a row? Then again, would it be so terrible if tonight's date doesn't show? I can enjoy a quiet supper alone, then go home and watch The Tonight Show on TV.

Looking at my watch, my date is already twenty minutes late. I know that's not considered late in some circles, but I'm not one to follow the *queen's time*.

The server startles me when he efficiently brings my bourbon and coke.

"Is there anything else I can get for you?" the server asks with a raised brow, noting the two menus and the empty chair across from me.

"It appears my dinner companion is running a bit late," I say, feeling the heat of embarrassment rising up the back of my neck. "Would you mind checking back in a few minutes?"

"Of course, sir," the server replies before walking away.

Taking a deep breath, I let out a sigh of relief before taking a sip of my drink. Whoa, this drink is strong! It's like all the liquor is floating on top. I grab the stirrer and mix my drink while checking out my surroundings. The floor is of worn linoleum with a stone-colored flagstone-like pattern. The walls are covered in a funky wallpaper depicting hanging baskets of begonias and stately trees, giving off a garden vibe. Well, mainly just the trunks of trees since the low ceiling cuts off their foliage. Scattered around the dining room are replica Greek statues perched on white plaster pedestals. The place has the feel of an outdoor Greek garden. Looking up at the ceiling, an imitation night sky is peeking through the painted leaves of arching treetops. Of course, the ceiling is just a regular flat ceiling. Still, it's painted to resemble an evening sky of stars and leafy treetops.

"Hello?" a timid voice comes from across the table.

Looking up, I see an anxious, tall, skinny guy. He appears a little bit older than me, with thinning dark hair that is probably dyed and huge black-framed glasses with coke bottle lenses that sit on a long, reddish nose. He's clean-shaven and dressed in a somber black suit like he will attend a funeral. He reminds me of the vampire date I'd had recently, but this guy's older and not wearing black eye makeup.

"Are you Mr. Shane?" he asks in a trembling voice.

"There's no need to be so formal; call me Shane," I reply, half-rising from my chair while extending my hand.

"I'm Edmond," he introduces himself and shakes with a thin, pale, unsteady hand.

I expect his hand to be damp and sweaty. And boy, am I right. It's wet and cold, like a day-old dead fish.

Edmond wipes his hand on a mysteriously appearing handkerchief while scrutinizing the empty chair.

Unfortunately, I'm not as fortunate. I smear Edmond's cold hand sweat onto my slacks.

"Please," I motion towards the empty chair. "Take a seat."

He pulls out the chair, slides into it, and anxiously surveys his surroundings.

"Have you been here before?" I inquire. Judging by his intense scrutiny of the restaurant, he probably hasn't. However, the question slips out before I'm able to retract it.

"Oh, no way," Edmond shakes his head, uncomfortably looking around like a lost tourist. "I don't get out much—because of my job. You know how that goes."

Silence ticks, ticks, ticks away.

"Have *you* been here before?" Edmond timidly asks.

I lie and say *no*, not wishing to go into detail about being stood up when I was here last evening.

Silence returns. Tick. Tick. Tick.

"If you don't mind me asking, what do you do for a living?" I ask the first thing that comes to mind to break the silence.

"I'm a funeral home embalmer," he says without emotion.

Ah, that explains his peculiar attire. I wonder if Edmond and Abacus might be better matches. Deep down, I know nothing will come of Edmond and me, romantically or professionally—I do not intend to be embalmed anytime soon.

A heavy silence hangs in the air, creating an uncomfortable atmosphere between my date and me. Tick. Tick. Tick. As the tension becomes nearly unbearable, the server comes to my rescue, shattering the silence.

"Excuse me, sir?" the server politely addresses Edmond. "What can I get you to drink?"

Edmond seems lost in thought, taking an eternity to decide. Finally, he breaks the stillness.

"I'll have whatever he's having," Edmond motions toward my glass of amber liquid.

"Very good, sir, a bourbon and coke," the server nods.

"No. No," an alarmed Edmond announces in a voice of newfound confidence. "Alcohol shall never touch these lips."

"Would you prefer a plain coke instead?" the server offers, trying to accommodate Edmond's preference.

"Sure," Edmond nods, content with his choice.

"Very good, sir, a coke it is," the server replies.

"No ice, please," Edmond adds.

"Yes, sir, no ice," the server gives Edmond a quick side-eye.

"Uh," Edmond hesitates, "Can I get an iced tea instead?"

"Iced tea?" the server asks.

"Sweet tea," Edmond changes his order. "I might as well shoot the works and go all out tonight. The sky's the limit."

"Sweet tea?" the server confirms.

"Yes. Sweet tea it is," Edmond smiles, clearly pleased with his final choice.

"Sweet tea," the server confirms. "Is that without ice?"

"Heaven forbid, young man," Edmond interjects, "it's not iced tea without ice."

"Yes, sir," the server says while giving Edmond a sidelong glance, then scurries off before my dinner companion changes his mind again.

I shake my head, utterly baffled at what I witnessed. I want to crawl under the table from sheer embarrassment for my date.

Silence again engulfs our table as we peruse our menus.

It's up to me to break the silence, but the server beats me to it by placing a tall glass of sweet tea on the table in front of Edmond.

"Can I take your order?" the server asks me, ignoring Edmond's presence.

I gesture for Edmond to give his order to the server.

Ignoring my gesture, Edmond continues to study the menu.

"Order whatever you want," I tell Edmond, hoping my offer will help him decide sometime tonight. "Dinner's on me."

"Sir?" the server prompts Edmond, trying to get his attention.

"Are you talking to me?" Edmond inquires, raising an eyebrow at the server.

"Yes, sir," the server responds, forcing a smile while clenching his teeth. "What can I get for you?" He holds an order pad and pencil, poised to jot down our choices.

"I'm not quite sure," Edmond hesitates, scratching his head. "There are so many choices; it's difficult to decide."

"Sir, may I suggest the chicken fried steak?" the server offers, attempting to get things moving along.

"Uh, well, I guess that'll do," Edmond concedes, shrugging his shoulders.

"Would you prefer a side salad or carrots?" the server asks.

"What kind of dressing comes with the side salad?" Edmond inquires.

"It comes with our exclusive house dressing," the server replies.

"I don't know. House dressings are always a gamble. You never know what you're getting," Edmond says, further examining the menu.

"How about a ranch dressing substitute?" the server chimes

in.

"Nah," Edmond shoots the waiter a sour expression, saying, "I'm not a big fan of ranch."

"What about french dressing?" the server suggests.

"Uh, I guess I could tolerate that," Edmond reluctantly agrees.

Turning to me, the server asks with a genuine smile, "And what can I get for you, sir?"

"I'll go with the roast chicken," I reply.

"Excellent choice, sir," the server nods, quickly jotting down my order on the pad.

"Can I possibly make a small substitution?" I ask. "May I swap the green beans for steamed broccoli?"

"No problem," the server assures, making a note on his pad.

"That's a chicken-fried steak and a house salad with french dressing substitute, and a roast chicken with steamed broccoli substitute?" the server confirms.

"Hmm, the roast chicken sounds tempting," Edmond hesitates. "Instead of the chicken-fried steak, would you please change my order to the roast chicken?" Edmond asks the server.

"Certainly, would you prefer green beans or steamed broccoli with that?" the server asks Edmond with a forced smile.

"Green beans—broccoli makes me gassy," Edmond says.

"So, that's two roast chickens, one with green beans and the other with steamed broccoli?" the server asks.

"Excuse me, I have a question," Edmond tells the server. "How are the green beans prepared? Are they steamed or boiled?"

"They're steamed," the annoyed server replies while tapping his pen on the order pad.

"Gotcha. Do you have peas?" Edmond inquires.

"Would you like to substitute your green beans for peas?" the frustrated server asks.

"Are they the big, bright green peas or the smaller, duller green ones?" Edmond inquires.

"They're the big, bright green ones," the server seethes through clenched teeth.

I half expect the waiter to give up and throw his hands in the air out of sheer irritation. I don't know how he manages to keep from screaming. My date is driving both me and the server crazy.

Edmond sits in silence, holding his mouth askew.

The server and I exchange glances, waiting for Edmond to speak.

"I think I'll go for the chicken fried steak," Edmond says, breaking the silence.

"Would you like the side salad or the carrots?" the server is eager to complete this order.

Edmond ponders briefly before responding, "I'll have the side salad, but with oil and vinegar dressing."

"So, just to clarify," the server says, "you want the roast chicken with steamed broccoli and the chicken fried steak with an oil and vinegar side salad?"

As the exasperated server scribbles down the corrections on his pad, his patience is obviously wearing thin.

The server and I look at Edmond, holding our breath, wondering if he will change his order again.

Edmond shoots a perplexing look at the server and then at me. "What's everyone looking at?" he asks, totally clueless.

CHAPTER 17

Date from hell

During my second year of junior high school, I had a girlfriend named Karen Taylor. We were what was called *going steady* because she wore my ID bracelet, and we were *going together*. Per the unwritten rules of junior high school etiquette, we were *an item*.

Every day after school, I'd walk Karen home and carry her books. I didn't say much during our walks; Karen was a chatterbox. I let her ramble on about whatever she pleased. I didn't feel the need to contribute to the one-sided conversation. Perhaps I wasn't paying attention to her gibberish. Regardless, I was definitely not the talkative one in our duo.

Karen was a huge FM radio fan and stayed up to date with the latest pop songs and artists. One day, she surprised me by calling the radio station and dedicating a song to yours truly. She excitedly urged me to tune in to the radio for a surprise. So, I stayed up late into the night, waiting for the big moment. Finally, the radio DJ announced Karen's dedication, and her gesture flattered me. However, simultaneously, I couldn't shake off the embarrassment of having my name broadcast to all the radio listeners. I guess a part of me wished she hadn't requested that dedication. You know?

She entered radio contests all the time. You know, the ones where you get a prize if you're the twenty-first caller? Well, Karen had a knack for winning those types of contests. Once, she won a dinner for two at a decently-priced restaurant in town. Naturally, she asked me, her boyfriend, to join her for the free dinner she'd won.

We got gussied up and went to the restaurant to claim Karen's winning dinner for two. Once seated at our table, Karen excitedly announced to the waitress about the two free meals she'd won. That waitress's smile disappeared faster than a snowflake in a Texas July. The waitress put on this fake smile, and her voice turned all sour-like. I had no idea what brought that on. I was just a school kid, you know? But hey, after we stuffed our faces, it hit me why that waitress had acted so weird. She probably thought we wouldn't leave her a decent tip, or any tip, since we were just a couple of junior high school kids who won two free dinners from some local radio show. And guess what? She was right. It wasn't till after the meal that I figured I was supposed to leave a tip since Karen treated me to a free dinner. It would be the right thing to do. You know? I'm not the sharpest tool in the shed when thinking on my feet. But hey, I didn't have the cash to leave the waitress. Honestly, I had no clue how much people tipped waitresses. I never saw my daddy tip when we went out to eat as a family. So, I guess you could say I was following in my daddy's footsteps—like father, like son.

Let's back up to when it was time to order our meal. Karen couldn't make up her mind. She kept changing her order, and the poor waitress had to keep erasing and rewriting on her order pad. Karen bombarded the waitress with a bunch of questions like: *How's the food cooked? Is it spicy? Does it have added salt?* You get the idea.

Not only was I embarrassed, but I was also embarrassed for Karen, and I'm sure the waitress was beyond frustrated. I bet she wanted to quit her job right there on the spot.

I ordered the fried chicken platter with a side salad, mashed potatoes with gravy, and steamed green beans for my meal. I was satisfied with my choice, mainly because it wasn't costing me a dime.

However, Karen was the exception. She relentlessly badgered the unfortunate waitress. Eventually, Karen ordered the chicken fried steak platter without alterations or substitutions.

When the waitress brought our meals, Karen complained to

the waitress that the baked potato was undercooked.

The waitress took the potato back to the kitchen.

However, when the potato returned, Karen complained that it was overcooked. Not stopping there, she also expressed dissatisfaction with the chicken fried steak and even with the green beans. Karen went as far as to return the salad because it had tomato slices. Apparently, she has a strong dislike for tomatoes.

The free dinner was a disaster, revealing a dark side of Karen I'd not seen before. There was no doubt about it: she was a total nightmare regarding food. I guess the lesson is to never *go steady* with someone until you see how they act when they order a meal at a restaurant.

The following day at school, I approached Karen and asked for my ID bracelet. I made it clear that our relationship was over.

"Fine by me," she snapped while removing the bracelet. She then forcefully slapped the ID bracelet in my hand.

"Just so you know, that cheap bracelet made my wrist turn green," she announced.

I considered being honest by telling her I got the bracelet for a quarter from a gumball machine. But why stir up more unnecessary drama? So, I kept my mouth shut. After all, Karen was the talker between the two of us.

Dale Thele

CHAPTER 18

Monday evening, November 22
Spanish Village Restaurant

Dexter and Joshua change up the restaurant where I meet my next date. Tonight, my date and I are meeting at the Spanish Village. At first glance, the place may not look like much, but let me tell you, their Tex-Mex cuisine is absolutely mucho grande (excuse my Spanish). Interestingly enough, I've been craving tortilla chips and guacamole for the past few days.

Spanish Village is a popular eatery on the edge of the gay bar district. It's out of the way from the other eateries. Don't get me wrong, Spanish Village isn't a gay business. It just happens to be close to the gay bars. Let me give you a quick rundown of the nearby gay bars. First up, we have The Crossing, which is a hookup bar. Then there's The Blue Flamingo. Honestly, I've never been there. I've heard it's a drag bar. They do drag shows, pageants, and stuff like that. Across the street, there's a country dance bar, which I think is called Country. Now, I'm not entirely sure if it's a gay bar, but hey, it's there in the mix of the gay bars. On the side street next to Country are these nondescript stairs that lead to the Chain Drive, a gay leather bar in the basement. You'd never suspect it's down there if you're not in the know. It's tucked away in an unlit side street—or at least that's what I've been told. I'm not a bar hopper, so I can't guarantee the accuracy of what I'm telling you. I've picked up bits and pieces of gossip from friends and acquaintances. You can grab a free weekly gay news rag to get a more accurate listing of local bars or check the Damron Guide—which I'm not sure if it's even published anymore. Years ago, gay bars used to sell the guide; ask a gay bartender if the Damron is still being published. If it is, they will sell you a copy if they haven't run out. And you might as well purchase a fresh bottle of poppers while there.

Anyway, back to Spanish Village, it's not a village. In fact, it's one single building nestled below the sidewalk. When you enter, you'll notice the windows are up high near the ceiling. So, while you're enjoying your meal, you'll view people's ankles and shoes as they stroll by on the sidewalk outside. The walls and floor are made of these massive rocks, giving the place a cave-like feel. It's almost like you expect to see moss growing on the walls. If you spot something growing, I'd highly recommend you not touch it—it's probably best you don't know what it is. You understand what I'm saying?

A mix of mustiness and freshly made tortillas permeates the air. Every day, without fail, they whip up corn and flour tortillas from scratch in their kitchen. It's like a little slice of heaven for your nose and taste buds.

Mind you, the place isn't exactly packed with customers at this time of the evening. It's still early for the lively gay crowd. There are a few straight couples and families enjoying their suppers. As for me, I'm sitting alone at a table, waiting for my date. All I know about him is that he'll be rocking a pink polo shirt. Well, that narrows it down to about half the gay population in the country, considering pink polos are all the rage right now.

So, let's see who walks through that door. I can't wait to find out.

I don't have to wait long when the door swings open, and in walks a man—and I use the term loosely. Picture this:

An upturned pink polo shirt collar.

A lightweight pale blue sweater draped over his shoulders and loosely tied in front.

Pressed Khaki pants.

Burgundy boat shoes sans socks.

And let's not forget the smokey-tinted aviator sunglasses he dramatically removes from his face to atop his head of feathered bleach-blond hair. You know, the same hairstyle as George

Michael's from the pop music duo WHAM?

Scanning the room, this guy poses like he's auditioning for a modeling gig. It's as if he expects everyone to drop their forks and bow to his supposed greatness.

Ugh, I can't stand such pretentious queens.

What a stroke of luck! He's most likely my mystery date. Oh, how fortunate I am! I think to myself. Can you hear the sarcasm in my voice? If not, you need to pay better attention.

As a polite gesture, I wave, hoping that I'm signaling the wrong pink polo. To my dismay, the guy glides across the room towards me, his hips swaying dangerously close to knocking over furniture and unsuspecting customers. *Oh dear*, I mutter quietly to myself, desperately seeking divine intervention.

"Gurrrl," he screeches in a high-pitched falsetto, dramatically dropping a soft leather shoulder bag beside the chair across from me.

"You must be Chane," he says.

"The name is pronounced *Shane*, spelled with an *S*," I interject, attempting to correct the pompous queen. However, my comment falls on deaf ears as the unnamed pink polo flamer remains unfazed.

He responds with a dismissive wave, loudly announcing, "The name's Royce." He says while extending a limp wristed hand under my nose.

Seriously? What does this swishy queen expect me to do with that dangling hand—kiss it?

Hesitant, I reluctantly reach out to shake the hand, only for him to grasp my first two fingers and give them a dainty wobble instead of a proper handshake. And to top it off, he confidently poses by resting his other hand on his out-thrusted hip.

I'm suddenly nearly knocked over by an olfactory tidal wave of Calvin Klein. *Obsession* is one of three types of gay fragrances. The first of the three types of colognes is so overpowering that it takes over a room before the wearer enters. And then there are those subtler fragrances that tickle your nose, making you smile, even though you have no idea why. Those are the ones that create a delightful aura around the person wearing them. But then those heavier colognes sneak up on you from behind. The scent explodes like an atomic bomb within moments, and the mushroom cloud spreads, overtaking the room. It's so strong that it makes people within a certain perimeter cough and eyes water, except for the person wearing it. I can definitely say that Royce's cologne falls into the latter category. Seriously, did he take a bath in the stuff?

I suppress the urge to gag. Don't get me wrong—I enjoy Obsession, but only in small doses. Unfortunately, Royce seems to have doused himself in it, making it impossible for me to smell anything but. I'll never purchase Obsession again after this date, even if it's the last cologne left at Bloomingdale's fragrance counter.

Royce and his cologne settle into the chair across the table with a dramatic flair like I've never witnessed before. I admit, I haven't spent much time with flamboyant gay men like Royce, or any for that matter. I don't mean to disrespect Royce as a person, but honestly, he's embarrassing the shit out of me.

Sitting across from me, Royce goes on and on about himself, using extravagant hand gestures that are overly effeminate. He completely disregards subjects that don't revolve around him. I can't say I'm bored, though. It's actually quite entertaining to watch him in action. It's like witnessing a mesmerizing display of butterflies—thousands of butterflies gracefully dancing in the air. This is the first time I've seen a display quite like this. Honestly, I should be selling tickets to this extraordinary, once-in-a-lifetime show.

"Mary, I gotta be honest from the get-go," he begins. "Just to give you a heads up, I take only the dominant role in intimate encounters. I am the one who initiates, and I have no interest in being on the receiving end. In other words, I'm a total *top* with no desire to *bottom*, and I'm not well with Pillow Princesses."

First, what does this flittin' fairy mean by saying he's a TOP? I would have never guessed him to be a pitcher, not in a million years. I bet you a hundred bucks her legs spread wider than the Grand Canyon before her back hits the mattress. Second, what on earth is a Pillow Princess? And third, why is he calling me Mary?

Immediately, I make it clear to Royce that this dinner date is not a lead-in to a casual hookup. Besides, what would we even do in such a scenario? We both identify as *bottoms*—I say that because there's no way he's a top, no matter what he says. Some rules in nature can't be broken, and this is one of them. With that said, there wouldn't be much that he and I could do except bump uglies, even if I were interested. Additionally, Royce tends to talk excessively, spewing words like a yard sprinkler. Some of the words he uses are unfamiliar, making me wonder what language he truly speaks.

"There was this one time when I met a clean queen in a bubble palace," Royce says. "You will never find me cruising those places—gag me with a spoon. When he and I met, I was washing something—probably a quilt or something. Anywho, he was a real beefcake. Normally, I don't go for Mexicans—I'm not a Salsa Queen, thank you very much. I had no intention of taking him back to my pad. That would've been grody to the max. So we did the nasty in the alley behind the bubble palace while some mangy tom cat watched on."

I'm trying to determine where his story is heading and if it even has a point. It's truly astonishing how this guy can ramble on without taking a breath. He keeps going and going without even pausing for the tiniest of breaths. Seriously, where's Guinness World Records when you need them?

"Then, from out of nowhere," Royce continues, "this unhinged bull-dyke is in my face, reading me the riot act—like it's not obvious that she and her lipstick lesbian girlfriend are u-hauling before they've come off their first date."

U-hauling? I want to ask what he means by that, but he doesn't break for a breath. Jeez, I'm terribly out of touch with the hip lingo. His mouth keeps running non-stop. I have to assume he must be addicted to listening to his own voice. Is there medication for diarrhea of the mouth, I wonder?

"Up comes this ginger bear and his otter cub," Royce says. "I think *woof* to myself, but I don't want either of them to get the impression I'm a chubby chaser. I'll let them eye fuck me, but I'm not into threeways or settling down in some vanilla gayborhood of Stepford house husbands."

Honestly, this Royce guy just doesn't shut up. I'm hungry and want to order something to eat before the nearby bars announce *last call* for the night. Can't this idiot hear my stomach rumbling? I just want to get up in his face and yell, *Hey, Queen, shut the fuck up*. But I'm too polite to do that, so I sit and listen to him prattle on as my stomach growls like a wild beast coming out of hibernation.

CHAPTER 19

Thursday morning, November 25
(Thanksgiving Day)
my condo

Joshua and Dexter are at the condo, each with their respective dates. Meanwhile, I'm stag at my own Thanksgiving soiree—flying solo without a dinner companion.

Dexter's date is an adorable nerd. He's attractive but much geekier than I imagine Dexter to be interested in—coke bottle lenses and all. But I'd never say that to Dexter's face. However, I don't see them having a long-term future together; I figure it's more of a physical attraction. By the way, Dexter's date goes by the name Birch. It makes me wonder about his parents. Seriously, who in their right mind names their kid after a tree? Hippies?

Joshua's date is a lovely girl named Willow, who goes by Willie. It's interesting how parents these days are naming their kids after trees. Speaking of which, there's a tree in the desert called the Joshua tree, so Joshua is named after a tree for all intents and purposes. I can't say it was intentional because I wasn't there when he was named. Since I don't know the circumstances, I'd best shut up about trees and names.

Speaking of Joshua, let me tell you, when it comes to preparing food, he and Dexter are about as helpful as melted ice cubes on a hot summer afternoon sidewalk. But hey, they make up for it by being absolute pros at devouring any amount of food you put in front of them. On the other hand, Willie is a whole different ballgame. You won't believe it, but she volunteers to lend a hand in the kitchen. I know. Right? It's like finding a unicorn in your backyard.

So, while Willie and I whip up the most delicious turkey

meal you can imagine, the three boys are in the living room, parked in front of the TV, eyes glued to the screen, soaking up the Macy's Thanksgiving Parade. And let me tell you, those parade hosts sure know how to keep things interesting. I overheard one say: *this year marks the 56th anniversary of the parade.*

That's over half a century of parades that wide-eyed kids, myself included, waited impatiently to see Santa bring up the rear of the parade—year after year.

Finishing the Thanksgiving meal, we're sitting around the table. I'm chewing the last bite of my slice of pumpkin pie, listening to the kids' chatter, and wondering what to do with the holiday leftovers. That is, assuming there are leftovers because those boys can put away the food. I was about the same when I was their age. Nowadays, I can't handle all those rich foods like I used to. If I tried, I'd spend the rest of the day nursing a tummy ache and sitting on the toilet.

"Mr. Davison," Willie says, "how come you don't have a boyfriend?"

Joshua elbows Willie while silently shaking his head *no*.

I'd not thought about it until now, but since Kip is no longer in the picture, I suppose the boys feel the need to protect me from other people prying into why I'm single. It's not like I'm the one who ended things with Kip. However, Joshua might be sensitive about Kip's incarceration, even though he's been tough through the whole ordeal and has kept his emotions in check. Regardless of what I think, I've been asked a question, and it would be impolite not to answer.

"Well, Willie," I start, "I had a boyfriend for a while, you know? He's actually Josh's dad. But a couple of months back, he was wrongly accused of some crimes. And, his lawyer hasn't been able to prove his innocence—yet. So, unfortunately, Josh's dad is stuck in prison until the attorney can sort things out."

"Oh, I didn't know," Willie murmurs, lowering her head. "I'm sorry for you, Mr. Davison, and for you too—Josh. I didn't mean to get into your personal business."

"It's alright," I reassure Willie. "Like you said, you didn't know."

"Nevertheless," she insists. "I shouldn't have asked such a personal question."

The conversation abruptly surrenders to silverware clinking against bone china plates as the kids silently enjoy their desserts.

"Mr. Davison," a curious Birch breaks the harsh silence. "I'm confused about how you're Dex's uncle, and Josh's dad was your boyfriend."

I pause, taking a deep breath, uncertain how to answer Birch's question. Our family isn't what most people would consider conventional, not by a long shot. You see, Dexter and Joshua are family to me. It may not fit the traditional mold, but it works for us. However, explaining this to someone outside our circle is a different story. Nevertheless, Birch has posed a question, and I must do my best to provide an answer.

"Well, let me explain..." I hem and haw, trying to figure out where to begin explaining our circumstances.

"Hold on a second," Dexter interjects, his eyes gleaming. "Uncle Shane isn't my blood relative, you know that, right? You see, he used to work with my mom, and that's how we originally met. Uncle Shane and I had this instant connection, and a great friendship came from that. It felt so natural that I started calling him *Uncle Shane*."

"Ah, I get it now," Birch chimes in, grasping the gist of the situation. "It's more like a nickname than a real family connection."

"Exactly, Birch," Dexter nods. "Uncle Shane is like a god-uncle."

Thanks to Dexter's quick thinking, we dodged a long and confusing explanation about how Joshua and Dexter found out they were half-brothers, Joshua finding out who his real dad is, and all the complicated details that come with our family coming together. Dexter's wit saved us from a tangled mess of a story.

"Hey, guess what? Uncle Shane's been dating," Dexter interrupts. His quick thinking saved us from the awkwardness of our guests figuring out our family details and bombarding us with more questions about our family ties.

"Really?" Birch asks, his eyes are wide in surprise.

"Is it that difficult to believe that an old geezer like me can go on dates?" I chuckle teasingly.

"Oh, no, sir," Birch responds, blushing and shyly tucking his head, revealing two adorable dimples.

At the moment, I understand why Dexter has feelings for this boy.

"Yeah," Dexter says. "Uncle Shane's gone on quite a few dates lately."

"I wouldn't call three dates *quite a few*," I quickly correct.

"Have you met anyone special?" Willie asks.

"No. Not so far," I say.

A hush falls over the condo. I can't help but feel responsible for this sudden silence, as if everyone is feeling sorry for my inability to find that special someone.

"You know what?" Willie pipes up. "I have an uncle who's gay. He's around your age, and he's single."

"I don't think I'd be comfortable going on a blind date set up by my nephew's girlfriend," I say.

"Hey, Uncle Shane, that might not be such a bad idea after all," Joshua adds.

"Thanks, Josh," Willie says, kissing his cheek.

"I'm not sure it's such a great idea," I protest.

"Come on, Uncle Shane," Dexter says. "It can't be any worse than the dates you've been on lately."

"You make a valid point," I say.

"Well then, it's decided," Willie says. "Leave it to me. I'll take care of everything. My uncle is a real catch, you'll see."

How did I agree to go on a blind date with Willie's uncle? No time to dwell on that; I've got a queasy stomach. Maybe I shouldn't have had that third slice of pie. Oh crap, do I have extra toilet tissue in the pantry?

CHAPTER 20

Wednesday evening, December 1
downtown restaurant

Unlike the previous blind dates where my date and I met indoors, Willie arranged for her uncle and me to meet outside a specific restaurant. Surprisingly, we both arrived simultaneously. It was easy to spot each other immediately, thanks to the red carnations we wore on our lapels. All credit goes to Willie for her romantic touch. Man, she knows how to set a mood for high expectations.

We get our introductions out of the way, right up front. Willie's uncle is named Ledger, which surprised me because I expected he'd be named after a tree. Instead of *Ledger*, he prefers to go by *LG*. I assume his middle name must begin with the letter G. However, it turns out his middle name is *Coltrane*. Naturally, my curiosity gets the best of me.

"Why do you go by LG?" I ask.

"If you want to know the truth," Ledger says, "this might sound a bit corny, but hear me out. When I was a kid, I started going by LG. Ledger sounded like an old man's name in my child's mind. After all, I was named after my granddad."

"I understand why you had apprehension about the name *Ledger*," I say, nodding in agreement.

"The story behind LG is quite simple," LG says. "When I split my name in half, the first letter of the first three letters is L, and the first letter of the last three letters is G. I put the two letters together. I thought LG sounded sophisticated. And that's where *LG* came from. I've been LG ever since."

LG and I had a pleasant supper, and afterwards, we took in a movie at the movie theater that everyone was talking about: *E.T.*

the Extra-Terrestrial. Then, we walked about downtown, taking in the Christmas lights. It was too warm and muggy to feel much like the holidays, but that's the gamble we take in Central Texas. Sometimes, it's chilly, and sometimes, it feels like Indian Summer, not wanting to give up the ghost. The evening was very conventional and lovely, but I didn't feel a romantic connection with LG. It seemed like I was out on the town with my brother—not a potential boyfriend.

Mutually, we agreed to chalk the evening up to a pleasant evening and part ways as friends, leaving the experience what it was—an enjoyable evening between friends. I tried to make things work between us, mainly for Willie's sake. However, contrary to romantic movie scripts, you can't force two people to come together and expect them to instantly fall in love. Sometimes, two people can have a great time together but still lack that spark needed to start a relationship. Relationships can't be rushed or forced; they have to develop naturally. Don't get me wrong, I liked LG very much, just not in a romantic way. You know what I mean? I'll know when I meet the right guy, and LG wasn't him, at least not for me, not right now.

Honestly, I don't think I was the right match for LG either. I still can't stop thinking about Griffen. Remember him? He was the first blind date the boys set me up with. He seemed perfect, and we got along so well. I was convinced he was my Mr. Right. I have no idea why I can't get him out of my mind. Although he discarded my phone number like it was trash, his memory still lingers. I just can't let go of the dream of a life with Griffen, even though I know it will never happen.

CHAPTER 21

Thursday morning, December 2
my condo

I wasn't excited about breaking the news to Willie, Joshua's girlfriend. She was a sweet girl, and she meant well by setting me and her uncle up on a date. However, things didn't work out between LG and me. As it turns out, Joshua had already moved on to a new girlfriend, leaving Willie behind as a ghost of Thanksgiving past.

Just so you know, I've grown accustomed to having the boys around the condo in the mornings and evenings. It's a great way to start and wrap up the day around the kitchen nook or the dining table. They're like stray cats—feed them once, and they keep returning. However, breakfast and supper are only guaranteed on weekdays. Saturdays and Sundays are questionable, as they might or might not show up for a meal. So, I cherish the weekday meals with the boys. Although I might grumble about them being underfoot, I don't mean any of it. I'd be lost without them.

"Tell us, Uncle Shane," Dexter says, sawing through a stack of breakfast waffles with a knife and fork. "When are we going to get the Christmas tree?"

"Christmas tree?" I ask, caught off guard. "It's barely December."

"But the stores are decorated," he insists.

"Yeah, man," Joshua adds. "They've had Christmas stuff out since before Thanksgiving. Downtown turned on the Christmas lights on Thanksgiving night."

"So," Dexter says, his mouth full of waffles, "we're falling behind."

"Why suddenly do you want to keep up with the Joneses?" I ask, raising an eyebrow. "And please, don't talk with your mouth full."

Dexter sheepishly wipes his mouth with a napkin, trying to act innocent.

"Who the heck are the Joneses?" Dexter asks, eagerly slicing another waffle into bite-sized chunks.

"Never mind," I say dismissively. "It's an old expression."

"Well?" Joshua asks impatiently. "When are we going to get a tree?"

"We'll discuss this again in a week or two, alright?" I say.

"Fine," Dexter grumbles, his voice dripping with indignation. "By waiting, all the good trees will be bought up."

"I'll take my chances," I reply with a snicker.

I know that the live Christmas trees haven't arrived yet. In previous years, Kip and I got our trees from a particular lot that doesn't open for another two weeks.

"Don't worry, guys," I say. "We'll find the perfect tree when the time is right."

"Go ahead, do whatever you want," Dexter taunts with heavy disappointment. "But don't come crying to me when you end up with a lousy *Charlie Brown* Christmas tree."

Here I am, playing the role of a grumpy old uncle to two teenage boys who aren't even related to me. It's funny how life turns out sometimes. At 26 years old, I never in my wildest dreams imagined I'd find myself looking after a pair of teenagers who won't be teenagers for much longer.

Suddenly, the phone rings, breaking the tension in the room.

Joshua lunges for the wall phone, but Dexter claims victory.

"Hello, Davison residence," Dexter announces smugly, speaking into the receiver.

Joshua retaliates by punching Dexter in the upper arm, clearly annoyed at being outmaneuvered.

Dexter grins from ear to ear, relishing in his triumph.

"Uncle Shane," Dexter says, holding his hand over the

receiver. "It's someone for you."

"Golly," I exclaim. "Really? A phone call for me? I wonder who would call me *here* and on *my* phone?"

"Alright," Dexter replies, but quickly adds in a hushed tone, "It's a man."

"Did he mention his name?" I inquire, mocking Dexter's soft tone.

"No," Dexter responds in a whisper. "But he sounds attractive."

"How can you tell if someone is attractive by their voice over the phone?" I ask, raising an eyebrow.

Dexter shrugs.

"Here, give me the phone," I say, taking the phone receiver from him.

"Hello," I say into the phone. "This is Shane."

There's a brief pause as I nod, but I remain silent, attentively listening to the person on the other end of the line.

"Uh-huh," I say, followed by a few more silent nods.

"Sorry," I say. "That's not it. But thanks for calling."

I hang up the phone and settle back into my bar stool at the breakfast nook.

"So?" Joshua asks, sitting on the edge of his stool. "How much longer are you going to keep us in suspense? Who was that?"

"Who?" I ask.

"That guy, just now, on the phone," Joshua says.

"Oh, him?" I dismiss the call altogether to drive the boys nuts. "It was nobody," I reply, calmly sipping my coffee and looking at the morning newspaper.

"Nobody?" Dexter questions. "It was a man. I distinctly heard his voice. He specifically asked for you—by name."

"Come on," Joshua begs, "ple-e-e-ase?"

"Uncle Shane," Dexter says, "please, spill the tea."

"Oh, alright, if you must know," I say, shrugging my shoulders. "It was a man calling about my stupid lost ring."

"Judging by your tone," Joshua says to me, "I'm guessing it

wasn't your ring after all."

"Nope," I reply. A tinge of sadness creeps into my voice as I gaze down at my naked pinkie finger.

"Don't worry, it'll turn up—you'll see," Joshua says, trying to inject some optimism into the situation.

"I'm afraid it's gone for good," I admit, my voice filled with resignation, feeling a sense of despair.

A heavy silence descends upon the kitchen. There's not much else to be said. When something of great personal value disappears, it's a bitter pill. Sometimes, you must accept that when something is lost—it's gone forever.

CHAPTER 22

Friday evening, December 3
Savoy Hotel

The Savoy Hotel is a luxurious and expensive establishment constructed in the late 1800s by a wealthy oil tycoon named Samuel B. Savoy. It offers a unique blend of historical charm and recently added modern amenities. Legend has it that the hotel is haunted by the spirits of past guests who died here. Personally, I'd rather not have to contend with ghosts; a blind date is enough to deal with for the time being.

I stroll into the swanky Savoy Hotel Restaurant, feeling all ritzy and whatnot. I'm early for my date, so I go to the bar to wait for him to show. I order a bourbon and coke, trying to look cool and sophisticated but feeling out of place in such a fancy hotel.

"Hey, guy, you Shane Davison?" a stranger asks as he sidles up next to me.

"Yes, that's me," I say with a guarded raised eyebrow. "Who, may I ask, wants to know?"

"I'm Henry—Henry Cullen—your date for the night," the man introduces himself with a sly grin.

I give him a puzzled look, unsure what to make of him.

"Oh, don't worry," he quickly adds. "The filly at the door pointed you out when I walked in. I promise I'm not some creepy stalker—unless that's your thing."

I sigh in relief, grateful I won't be sharing a meal with some crazy person. We exchange handshakes, and he orders himself a drink.

As we get comfortable at the bar, we're informed our table is ready.

A waitstaff whisks us away to a table in the dining room.

"So, Mr. Davison," Henry inquires as we're seated at our table, "what do you do for a living?"

"Please, call me Shane," I reply. "To answer your question, I'm a Financing Broker."

"Is that similar to an Investment Banker?" Henry asks.

"You could say the two professions are similar," I respond, not wanting to bore him with the details of my chosen career path.

"And you," I inquire, my tone laced with curiosity. "What is it that you do?"

"I'm afraid I'm not involved in anything quite as interesting as you," Henry chuckles lightly. "I'm a traveling salesman by trade."

I figure he must be doing well to afford Austin's most expensive hotel. Of course, I could ask what he sells, but I'm not interested in what he's peddling. Besides, traveling salesmen are not typically the type of men to seek stability and commitment. I assume I'm in for a long, boring evening, and we haven't even placed our supper orders yet.

"So, where is your home base?" I ask, attempting to salvage the situation by mustering up some feigned interest. "I'd love to know more about your travels." I might as well try to make the most of the evening since I have nowhere else to be.

"I'm based out of Dallas," he says, his voice filled with a hint of exhaustion. "I spend a couple of days in Fort Worth, a couple in San Antonio, and a day or two here in Austin."

"That must be tough," I reply, trying to sound sympathetic. "Living out of a suitcase, going from one hotel to another."

"It's not so bad," he says, surprisingly upbeat. "I get to meet a lot of interesting people."

"I can imagine," I say, pretending to be interested. I finish my drink and scan the room for a server. I'm eager to order my meal and wrap up this evening as swiftly as possible.

Without missing a beat, Henry gulps down the remainder of his drink in one swift motion.

"I'm not really all that hungry," Henry casually remarks.

"How about we take this party up to my room?"

Wait, did he ask what I think he asked?

"Um, I, uh..." I stumble over my words, unsure of how to respond. "I'm afraid you've misconstrued the intent of the evening."

"What exactly are you trying to say?" Henry curiously asks.

"Well, you see..." I say, trying to gather my thoughts. "This evening was meant to be a proper date, not a casual hookup."

"We can call this whatever you want," he says, rising from his chair. "Let's continue this upstairs in my room, shall we?"

"No, no, no," I quickly interject. "You've got this all wrong. I'm not looking for a quick fling."

"You're not interested in hooking up?"

"That's not what I'm looking for," I say.

"Looks like we got our wires crossed," he says, his voice tinged with disappointment.

"Yeah, it seems that way," I reply, trying to keep the conversation light. "I suppose this is where I say *good night.*"

"You don't have to leave so soon," he suggests with a hint of hope. "You're cute as a button, and the invitation to come to my room is still open," he winks, and his lip curls suggestively.

I shake my head *no* and place some bills on the table. Despite not staying long enough to eat a meal, I leave more than enough cash to cover my drink and a generous tip.

"Well," Henry says, smirking. "Have it your way. You're missing out on a damn good time."

"Maybe so," I reply, maintaining my composure. "But I'm declining your offer, regardless." I turn from the table, refusing to look back. A sense of unease overwhelms me, even though I've done nothing wrong. The mere thought of what Henry had in mind infuriates me. Why can't two men go on a simple dinner date without there being expectations of more? Is something inherently wrong with just wanting to spend time getting to know one another and maybe falling in love?

I want to go home and take a long shower to wash away the nightmarish memories of this evening.

What will I tell the boys when they ask about my date? I guess I'll lie and tell them I got stood up again. Even I can believe that one.

CHAPTER 23

Monday evening, December 6
35th Street Diner

Joshua and Dexter are more determined than ever to find me a boyfriend before Christmas. They have less than three weeks remaining to meet their self-imposed deadline. They'll need a good old-fashioned Christmas miracle to meet this deadline. Hoping for divine intervention, they set me up for yet another blind date.

This time, my date and I are meeting at the 35th Street Diner instead of some fancy restaurant. Let me tell you, this place is a real hidden gem. It's a small, old-school joint that's been around for ages. You'd only stumble upon it if you actively searched for it. I'm trying to figure out how Joshua and Dexter discovered the place.

Entering the diner is like taking a nostalgic trip back to the 50s. Considering my only point of reference are TV shows and movies, I was a little kid during the latter part of that era. The entire place is adorned with shiny chrome fixtures and vinyl seat covers. They even have a fully functional jukebox in the front corner, which is pretty cool. You can perch on bar stools at the counter or settle into a cozy booth beside the front windows. As luck would have it, I snag a booth right in the center.

The tables are covered with faded red and white checkered plastic tablecloths. It seems they're trying to achieve that classic cotton look but with the added bonus of easy cleaning. As I look up toward the ceiling, I notice large, globe-shaped light fixtures suspended by chains, giving the place a nostalgic feel. Some of the chains even appear to be rusty, probably due to leaks in the roof. Taking a peek over the top of the counter and bar stools, a cubbyhole opening in the wall allows a glimpse at the chef hard at work in the kitchen; a radio plays somewhere beyond the window-like opening in the wall. The clattering of pots and pans nearly drowns out the radio program.

A middle-aged waitress sashays to the booth, wearing a pale blue waitress uniform that looks straight out of an old TV show. Nowadays, you don't see women dressed like that, especially wearing a beehive hairdo. Still, she has a white ruffly apron tied around her waist and a plastic name badge displaying her name, *Lola Mae.* She's even sporting white nylons and those classic nurses' lace-up shoes. She sets a red translucent plastic glass of ice water on the table. Then removes a triple-fold laminated menu from under her arm. Handing it to me, she flashes a quick smile.

"Can I get ya sumpin' to drink, shugur?" Lola Mae asks with a thick accent, one that's distinctively southern.

"Do you have sweet tea?" I inquire.

"Shure do, hon, but take it frum me. Order the regular iced tea and add the shugur yerself," she suggests, swaying her hip from side to side.

Considering her age, I wonder if she's breaking in a newly installed hip.

"Regular iced tea it is," I reply, expressing my gratitude with a smile. "By the way, someone will be joining me."

"Shure thing, sweetie, I'll bring ya another water and a menu," she promises before walking away, hip-swiveling like it's just been freshly lubed.

As I wait for my dinner companion, my gaze remains fixed on the door. All I know about my date is that he's an accountant, and I'll spot him by a yellow scarf.

Meanwhile, I straighten the knife, fork, and spoon on the table before me. Then, I focus on the sugar dispenser, salt, and pepper shakers. I'm not entirely sure if it's nerves or my OCD tendencies. Still, I feel this irresistible urge to align these table accessories precisely to my preference.

The jingle of a small bell attached over the door jingles like crazy.

All the diners swivel their heads to look at the person coming through the door.

He's wearing a bright yellow scarf wrapped snugly around his neck. He bears a striking resemblance to the Ichabod Crane character from Washington Irving's *Sleepy Hollow*. This tall and lanky guy sports a pair of dainty round wire-frame glasses.

The customers return to their meals and conversations until the next person sets the small bell to jingling.

I wave to get the man's attention.

He nods and walks awkwardly towards the booth.

"Good evening," he says in a cold and business-like tone. "I'm Cornelius. You must be Shane?" He extends a long, slender hand for a weak handshake.

"Please, have a seat," I say, motioning to the empty bench across from me.

Cornelius scoots across the vinyl upholstered bench, and in doing so, a noticeable fart-like sound comes from his side of the table.

Horrified, he freezes in place with a wide-eyed expression.

"Pardon me," he says, ducking his head.

The situation could not be more uncomfortable. What do I say? I don't for a minute believe that was a bodily sound. It was probably the squeal of the vinyl. But then again, I could be mistaken. Unsure of what to say, I shrink behind my menu.

Thank god, just in the nick of time, Lola Mae returns with a glass of water, another menu, and a fresh set of stainless steel utensils wrapped in a paper napkin.

Cornelius begins wrestling with his long overcoat, squirming in the booth as he works to wriggle out of the coat. After a fierce struggle, he emerges victorious.

I should add that it's early evening, and the sudden plummet in temperature caught everyone off guard. Folks had little warning they'd have to rummage through their closets in search of cold-weather apparel. These brief and sudden cold snaps are rare and inconvenient since we're accustomed to typically mild Texas winters. Who'd have thought we'd need heavy coats this evening when, at lunchtime, it was in the mid-80s? That's Texas unpredictable weather for you—go figure.

After carefully folding his woolen coat, Cornelius places it beside himself on the bench. A few minutes later, he snatches the coat, rummaging through the pockets as if he's misplaced something of incredible value.

"Have you lost something?" I inquire.

"Yes," he says sharply, his eyes filled with terror. But then, a wave of relief washes over him as he produces an inhaler from a coat pocket. Swiftly, he brings the device to his mouth and presses the button twice, taking a deep breath. He exhales with renewed relief before slipping the inhaler back into his coat pocket.

"Are you okay?" I ask.

"Nothing to worry about, just a touch of asthma," he replies.

Well, that's a relief. I can't imagine what I'd have done if Cornelius said it was a severe case.

As the evening progresses, the date and the outdoor temperature plummet downward. He searches more frequently for his inhaler, taking two puffs to breathe before the onset of the next attack. I worry about Cornelius, a man I barely know, fearing that he might have a major attack and drop dead at the table. In my mind, I picture the paramedics asking about my date and me unable to answer them. All I'm sure of is a dead body named *Cornelius* is slumped across the table in the window booth as I slurp my iced tea.

Cornelius, whose last name I don't recall him ever revealing, is a total bore. He hardly adds anything to our conversation, leaving me to do all the questioning and him responding with a mere nod or shake of his head. All I want is for him to return to the storybook pages, where he belongs alongside the headless horseman so that I can get on with my life.

So, what's wrong with me? Why can't I find a decent gay guy

who has his shit together or at least part of it? Is there something about me? Or have I set my expectations too high? Has the dating scene become more complicated since Kip and I dated? Honestly, I'm feeling disheartened, ready to throw in the towel and embrace the single life forever and ever. You know what I mean?

CHAPTER 24

Wednesday early evening, December 8
Luby's Cafeteria

The boys caught me off guard when they said I'd meet my next blind date at Luby's Cafeteria. I mean, Luby's? That place hasn't crossed my mind in years. I remember when I was in high school, and we went to out-of-town speech and drama contests, Luby's was our go-to place for lunch if we were lucky enough to find one. You see, our hometown didn't have a cafeteria except the one at the school. So, eating at Luby's was like hitting the jackpot when we were out of town. Now, I can't help but feel a wave of nostalgia coming on for this upcoming date. Even if the date is a dud, at least it'll bring back some good ol' high school memories. Go Badgers!

I arrive at Luby's and wait in this small lobby for my blind date to arrive. I'm early because of the changing weather, getting a head start on the incoming rain, and it's darn chilly outside. I don't want to catch a cold. Luckily for me, this little lobby provides some shelter from the elements.

Joshua and Dexter didn't give me much to go on about the guy I'm meeting, except that he's a Realtor and will wear a red blazer. I wish I could remember the name of the Realtor who sold Kip and me our condo. I recall he wore a red blazer and was a hardcore salesman, dead set on getting us to sign a contract. If I'm not mistaken, he had sandy blond hair and a strangely tanned complexion, considering it was winter. I can't recall his name, and now I wonder if the guy I'm meeting is the same. When Kip and I viewed the condo, my gaydar went off—I didn't doubt that our Realtor was gay.

I'm abruptly jolted out of my thoughts when a small boy

collides with my leg.

"Derrick, what do you say to the gentleman?" a man, whom I assume is the boy's father, asks him.

"I'm thorry, mith-ter," the boy mumbles, avoiding eye contact.

"No problem, there wasn't any damage," I reply, kneeling to meet the boy's gaze. "Little man, what's your name?"

"Dur-ick," the boy stammers, looking at me from behind his dad's pant leg.

"Well, Dur-ick," I say with a warm smile. "It's a pleasure to make your acquaintance." I offer to shake the boy's hand.

With a noticeable gap in his front teeth, the boy ducks behind his dad's leg.

"My son tends to be a bit standoffish around strangers," the man explains. "But once he warms to you, be prepared; he'll talk your ear off."

"You have an adorable son," I comment, rising upright.

"I'm Dirk Gibson," the man introduces himself, extending his hand.

I shake the offered hand in return.

"I apologize for Derrick running into you," Dirk apologizes. "My son tends to get overly excited and fails to watch where he's going."

"No problem," I say, crouching again to the boy's level. "Dur-ick, I'm delighted we ran into each other. It's been a pleasure meeting such a fine young man as yourself."

"Thank you," Dirk responds, smiling down at his son. "Button your coat, buddy. It's chilly and wet outside. We don't want to catch a cold, do we?"

The boy nods, quickly fastening his coat with tiny, chubby fingers.

"It was a pleasure meeting you," I say to Dirk.

"Likewise."

A gust of chilly wind blows into the lobby as the dad and son leave through the open door, causing a shiver to run down my spine.

Damn it, why didn't I wear a coat? I scold myself for the oversight.

It couldn't have been more than a few minutes when I notice a well-dressed man in a red blazer scurrying across the parking lot. I hold open the door for him, extending a warm welcome.

"Are you my date?" I inquire, introducing myself.

"Nice to meet you," replies the man with an oddly tanned complexion and sandy blond hair. "I'm Bradly McKenna, but everyone calls me Brad."

I can't believe it. This is the same guy who sold Kip and me our condo. I'm sure of it. When he said *everyone calls me Brad,* that's when I knew it was him. That's how he first introduced himself to Kip and me. It's a small world, isn't it? He doesn't remember me, but that's fine. Without wasting time, we head inside, where it's warm, and we walk through the cafeteria line, filling our trays with dishes and plates of food.

A few minutes later, we're seated at a table near a window. The sky outside is getting darker as the evening transitions into night. The lights in the parking lot flicker on, momentarily casting an orange glow over the cars below. A misty drizzle falls as the lights grow brighter, resembling snowflakes gently descending from the sky. The wintry scene outside gives me a cold shiver.

"Are you chilly?" Brad asks, breaking the silence.

"Nah, I'm good," I reply. "Just noticed how cold it looks out there..."

"I feel you," Brad nods. "This weather screams fireplace and hot cocoa, doesn't it?"

"Exactly," I say, trying not to give him the wrong idea. Agreeing on the weather doesn't mean I'm looking for an after-dinner hookup. Am I right?

Finished with my meal, I stack my dirty dishes like at home. Some habits you can never shake.

"So, how long have you been in real estate?" I ask Brad,

trying to make conversation.

"Been hustling the real estate game for a while now," he wipes his mouth with a napkin. "By the way, how did you know I'm a Realtor?"

"The blazer totally gives you away," I chuckle, pointing to his jacket.

"Yeah," Brad nods a sheepish smile, "I forget I'm a walking billboard in this flashy red sports jacket. There's no secret as to who my employer is."

As our conversation continues, Brad's pager beeps, demanding his attention. He swiftly unclips it from his belt and glances at the message. His face fills with a mix of curiosity and urgency.

"Sorry, I got to take this," he apologizes, rising from his chair to make a beeline for the pay phones at the building entrance.

After what feels like an eternity, Brad returns, settling back into his chair, ready to resume our conversation.

"You know, it's been ages since I've been to a Luby's," he says, looking around the dining room.

I nod in agreement. A bit of nostalgia creeps into my mind's eye.

"Me too," I say. "The last time I've been to a Luby's had to have been in high school."

"I reckon it's pretty much the same for me," he says. "The food hasn't changed one iota."

"Is that a good or a bad thing?" I ask.

"All good," he says. "Luby's is where my dad, mom, and sister celebrated special occasions, like birthdays and school accomplishments. Can't believe it's been so long since I've been here."

"I remember when—" Brad's buzzing pager cuts me off. "Go ahead and take that."

"Excuse me, I'll be right back," he says, rising from the table and heading towards the payphones.

A few minutes later, he returns.

"Is everything alright?" I ask, concerned about the situation.

"Work. Work. Work," he sighs, taking a sip of iced tea. "It never ends."

Observing the constant interruptions, I wonder how many more distractions I'll have to endure before the evening ends. Getting to know each other is complicated when his beeper keeps going off. I wonder what kind of life it would be with Brad if a beeper rules his life.

Speaking of a beeper, Brad apologizes while glancing at his again.

"I'm sorry, I need to take this," he says.

Left alone at the table, my interest in Brad wanes, and I impatiently await his return.

"I'm really sorry about this," Brad apologizes, his voice tinged with urgency. "But I've got to run. Work, you know."

"No worries," I reply, trying to sound disappointed.

"It's been real," Brad says in a rushed tone. "Maybe we can do this again soon? Oh, and don't hesitate to call me if you have any real estate needs." He swiftly drops one of his business cards on the table.

"Sure," I mutter, observing him darting towards the exit as if a fire has broken out.

Well, at least I didn't have to devise some lame excuse to end our date prematurely. Brad did a satisfactory job of that on his own. I grab the check and go to the cashier, feeling relief and annoyance over a date that started out great but turned into a train wreck much too early.

In the two times I've encountered Brad—the Realtor—it's cost me something. However, this time, the price of two Luby meals seems way more favorable than that of a brand-new luxury condo.

Standing at the checkout counter, the cashier drops a paper receipt and loose change into my palm. In turn, I drop the coins in a dish with random coins—you know, those need-a-penny-leave-a-penny dishes. If someone doesn't have enough change, they can help themselves to the coins in the dish.

I press the *Push* button on the metallic dispenser next to the cash register, and I'm rewarded with a toothpick in return. With a nod to the cashier, I bid her a good night as I pick at my teeth with the wood pick while making my way to the exit.

Another date, another disaster. I wonder if I'll ever meet *Mr. Right*? So far, I've met only *Mr. Wrongs*. I wish Kip were here; he was my *Mr. Right*.

CHAPTER 25

Saturday morning, December 18
Christmas tree lot

Yes, it turns out I'm just an ol' softy. I caved and took the boys' Christmas tree shopping. To be perfectly honest, they wore me down a little each day with their nagging and belly-aching. Boys can be a handful. You know what I'm saying?

The day started at the Christmas tree lot. The boys spent forever searching the lot, arguing and debating over practically every tree. You'd have thought they were negotiating world peace by how seriously they searched for the perfect tree. Eventually, the boys agreed on a live tree. I swear, those boys scoured the entire lot until they found the most expensive tree. But seeing the excitement on their faces was worth the money spent. My contribution consisted of writing the check for the tree and the addition of a live pine wreath I chose. The wreath was my idea to make my condo door look more festive.

It's funny how the holidays bring out the kid in all of us. Maybe it's the anticipation, the glittery greeting cards, the presents wrapped in colorful paper, or just the magic of Christmas itself. It's a shame the holiday feeling doesn't stick around once the crumpled wrapping paper is tossed away and the decorations are packed and stored for another year.

Anyways, let's get back to the live tree. We brought that beauty home and set it up in the living room. I suggested we let the tree rest for a few days before decorating it. But, oh no, the boys were itching to decorate it immediately So, we made numerous trips to and from the basement storage, hauling crates of holiday decorations upstairs to the condo.

We started trimming the tree once we had all the crates stacked in the living room like a warehouse. All the while, we sipped on hot cocoa and savored mouthwatering holiday cookies that I snagged from a nearby bakery on our way home. The air was filled with festive holiday music from the stereo and the scent of a live Christmas tree, which set the perfect mood. Honestly, the boys were bursting with excitement. I even turned down the thermostat to make it feel like Christmastime. It's funny; we wore shorts and tee shirts earlier in the day, enjoying the glorious 84-degree sunshine while searching for the perfect tree. You see, the weather in Austin during the winter holidays is always unpredictable. Most of the time, it's mild and sunny, but every now and then, we get a pleasant surprise with a chilly day, and that's when we dream of a white Christmas. But let's be real: the only surefire way to experience a white Christmas in Austin is by turning down the air conditioning, snuggling on the couch with a blanket, and watching snowy holiday movies on the boob tube.

Last month, I was anxious about the approaching Christmas season. But now that it's almost here, I've realized I stressed for no reason. This year is the boys' first Christmas without their dads, and I'm determined to make it absolutely fantastic for them. However, things may turn out better than anticipated. The boys are going all out, putting in a ton of effort to make this holiday season one for the ol' memory book.

I suppose I should bring you up to speed on my dating life. I've made the decision to call off the boyfriend search. I feel I've let the boys down. They were really hoping I'd find someone before Christmas. But hey, fate had a different plan for me. But don't fret; having the boys around during the holidays is more than sufficient. After all, the holidays don't feel complete without family, and the boys provide all the *family* I need to enjoy a great holiday season.

CHAPTER 26

Sunday evening, December 19
my condo

With Christmas just a week away, there's a ton of stuff to do and so little time. I mean, seriously, it's like a never-ending to-do list. Grocery shopping, buying gifts, wrapping them, writing and sending Christmas cards, and attending holiday parties. It all happens at once.

Anyway, I'm getting dressed for one of those aforementioned parties. I wear cotton boxer undershorts and dress socks when I step in front of the master bedroom vanity sink. I'm looking at my reflection in the mirror—deciding if I need to shave or not. Suddenly, I sense water soaking through my socks. Talk about an unexpected holiday surprise.

Curious, I bend down to investigate the situation. Opening the cabinet doors under the sink, what do I find? Water. Everywhere. It's like a mini flood pouring from the cabinet. The only thing missing is a tiny ark and Noah with all his paired animals. I switch from get-ready-for-party mode to a mission of finding the source of the leak. But let me tell you, the lighting under the cabinet is absolutely horrendous. I can barely see a thing. And let's be honest here: I'm not a plumbing expert. I'm clueless when it comes to anything about plumbing.

So, I'm standing in my underwear and wet socks, deciding what to do next. It's a Christmas crisis that requires calling in the professionals. On top of that, I'm late to a holiday party.

I phone building maintenance to report the leak.

Being that it's Sunday evening, I get the answering service instead of a live person. Frustrated, I leave a frantic message explaining that my condo is flooding due to a massive leak in the bathroom, like my own Niagara Falls. Can you blame me for exaggerating a little? I'm not losing my mind, but I'm definitely freaking out.

Amid the chaos, I stumble upon the shutoff valve under the sink and turn off the water to the vanity faucets. Phew! Crisis averted, at least for now. But here's the catch—without running water in the master bedroom sink, I have no choice but to use the guest bathroom until the leak is fixed. Also, I'm not all that keen on wading through puddled water. Talk about a pain-in-the-ass inconvenience.

Since it's late Sunday, I'm pretty darned sure I won't see anyone from building maintenance until tomorrow. I convince myself that I can tough it out till then. It's not a pressing matter that the repair is done this very minute. It's not like I have house guests occupying the guest bedroom. Besides, the water leak hasn't turned my place into a swimming pool, so I can handle a minor water inconvenience till tomorrow. Or, so that's what I tell myself.

I gather all the necessary toiletry items from the master bathroom and tote them to the guest bath. I then proceed to finish getting ready in the guest bathroom. However, as expected, I forget some of what I need and run back and forth between the two bathrooms. It's absolutely insane how we tend to overlook everyday conveniences until something as minor as a leaky pipe disrupts our daily routines.

Seriously, where did I put my toothbrush?

CHAPTER 27

Monday morning, December 20
my condo

The phone rings.

Frantic, I scramble for it as if tackling an opponent dashing to the end zone for a touchdown.

"Hello?" I say into the receiver, trying to sound composed.

Eating their breakfast, Joshua and Dexter sit at the breakfast nook, amused by my phone dance.

"Yeah, it would be great if you could send someone over here ASAP," I say eagerly into the phone. "Uh-huh. Thanks!" I end the call with a satisfied grin.

"Was that the building management company?" Dexter asks.

"Yep, thank goodness," I reply. "I'm getting my bathroom sink fixed today."

"I'll never understand why adults make such a fuss over a little water leak," Joshua says, shaking his head.

"Well," I chuckle, "one day you'll be an adult too, and it'll all make perfect sense."

Joshua shakes his head, swirling his half-eaten biscuit in the remnants of his runny, over-easy egg.

Knowing a plumber is on the way to fix the leak is a huge relief. Unfortunately, I wasn't given a specific time to expect him. I don't want to miss him, so I call my office and tell my assistant *I'm not coming in today because I'm waiting at home for a plumber. In my absence, I instruct my assistant to reschedule my appointments, and any urgent matters can be handled by someone else in the office.* Ah, the perks of being the boss. There's no need to devise a lame excuse when I'm not coming to work. It takes me back to when I worked at Dillinger's

Department Store. Back then, I had to get creative with my reasons for calling out. I don't know how I got away with some of those excuses, but somehow they did the trick.

Morning turns into noon, noon into the afternoon, the afternoon is edging on the evening, and I'm still waiting for the plumber.

At 4:36 p.m., the doorbell rings.

Bursting into action, I rush to the door and swing it open.

I don't give a flip what the plumber's name is or what he looks like; I only want my sink fixed.

"I'm here to fix a leak," he says.

I grab the plumber's arm, dragging him and his toolbox through the condo and into the master bath. I fling open the cabinet door and point to where yesterday, there was water, where water wasn't supposed to be.

Kneeling on the floor before the vanity, armed with a flashlight, *Mister Plumber* examines the troublesome pipe. He shines the light beam up and down the silver-colored pipe, searching for abnormalities.

"I'm not seeing a crack in the pipe," he says, scratching his head. "I'll have to open the valve to find the source of the leak."

With determination in his eyes, he slides his upper body into the cramped cabinet and twists the shut-off valve open.

"DAMN!" he exclaims, head and shoulders emerging from the cabinet. His hair is plastered to his head, water cascades down his chin, and his uniform shirt is soaked. "That's not what I intended," he chuckles, pulling a rag from his back pocket, then wipes the water off his face. "That's one sensitive valve. I barely turned it, and water sprayed everywhere."

"Did you see where it's leaking?" I ask while handing him a bath towel to dry himself.

"Actually, I did," he says, wiping his face with my plush towel. "It's not going to be a big deal to repair."

"If you take off your shirt, I can run it through the dryer for you," I say after seeing his wet shirt.

"Thanks," he hesitates, "I don't want to be a bother."

"No bother at all," I reassure him. "Plus, you don't want to wear a wet shirt for the rest of the day, right?"

"I guess you've got a point," he concedes. "Are you sure this isn't an inconvenience?"

"Hand me your shirt, and I'll dry it while you fix my leak," I say, trying to make things easier for the both of us.

I'm at a loss for what to call *Mister Plumber*, not knowing his real name. Honestly, I wasn't exactly thrilled about engaging in a conversation when he introduced himself upon arrival. I mean, I wasted my entire day waiting for him. But now, *Mister Plumber* is soaked, thanks to my leaky pipe. The least I can do is offer to dry his shirt. Of course, that means he has to take it off.

As he unbuttons the shirt, I notice he's not wearing an undershirt. My eyes immediately go straight to his defined chest. And I see he's wearing a chain around his neck with a pendant dangling from it.

"What's the pendant?" I ask, trying not to stare at his gorgeous chest.

"Oh, this?" he says, grasping the object dangling from the chain. "It's a ring. I came across it and hope to one day find its rightful owner."

"A ring, you say?" I inquire, my interest growing.

"Yes, I believe the owner lost it at the Policeman's Ball this past autumn."

"Why do you say that?"

"I met a gentleman who wore a ring just like this one," the plumber reveals. "Well, we didn't exactly exchange names..."

"Would you mind if I take a look?" I ask, eager to examine the ring.

He opens the necklace clasp, removes the chain from his neck, slides the ring off, and hands it to me.

I examine it closely. There's no doubt: this is my lost ring. But how can I convince him of that?

"If I remember correctly," I say, hoping to convince him I'm the ring's owner. "Weren't you dressed as a swashbuckler with a mask you didn't remove? You signaled for me to dance with you, but I declined. Yet, you insisted until I accepted your invitation."

"Could it be, after all these months, I've found you?" he asks. "There's one thing that can prove if you're the rightful owner of the ring."

"What's that?" I ask.

"Kiss me," he says.

"Kiss you? How will that prove anything?"

"Come on, humor me, please?" he insists.

Leaning in close to the man I've dreamt of, our lips meet. The kiss starts tentatively and builds into a passionate embrace, and our bodies press tight against each other.

"It's really you," he says with a wide grin as he pulls away.

"How can you be so sure?" I inquire.

"Because your kiss tastes of Dentyne chewing gum," he declares, licking his lips.

"That's my favorite gum," I admit.

He plucks the ring from my open palm and slides it onto my finger.

"Now, the ring is where it belongs, on the finger of its rightful owner," he declares.

I intently study the plumber's face, trying to place where I've seen those eyes. They seem oddly familiar; those are the same eyes I admired from behind a mask at the Policeman's Ball. But I've seen them somewhere else, somewhere more recently.

"We've met before, other than the Policeman's Ball, haven't we?" I inquire, unable to contain my curiosity.

"You remember?" He says with a hint of surprise flickering across his face.

"I'm not sure, but something feels strangely familiar," I say, eager to unravel the mystery.

"It wasn't long ago at Chez Pierre Ristorante. We met on a blind date. My goatee was shorter at the time," he reveals as a smile plays on his lips.

"Griff?" I gasp, my heart suddenly racing with a mix of

excitement and disbelief.

He nods.

Indeed, it is him. The realization hits me like a lightning bolt, and my heart, which had just returned to its regular rhythm, now beats faster than before.

"The one and only," *Mister Plumber* declares. "I had a fantastic evening with you, and I thought you did too—"

"I did."

"But what happened?"

"After we left the restaurant, I realized I'd left my business card case on the table. I went back to retrieve it. And guess what? I found the card I'd given you with my phone number lying on the floor next to the table." I say through welling tears and hurt memories that split open my heart.

"That's where that card went," he says, with a mix of frustration and regret. "When I got home, I searched every pocket, over and over again, desperately trying to find your card. I wanted to call you. But, unfortunately, I never found the card with your phone number."

A wave of relief washes over me, and I wipe away tears that involuntarily formed in my eyes.

"All this time, I thought you didn't want to see me again," I confess, my voice trembling.

"Since the night of our dinner date," he says. "I've wanted to call you," he admits; his words carry a hint of vulnerability.

A bittersweet smile forms on my lips.

"I've come to realize an undeniable truth," I say. "It's funny, no matter how badly we mess up, fate brings us back to who we are supposed to be with. You know, it's incredible how things work out sometimes. But I'm thrilled we found our way back to each other."

Picture this: my bedroom, where I unexpectedly reunited with the man who haunted my dreams. It all started when we bumped into each other incognito at a fancy fundraising shindig. Talk about a chance encounter. But apparently, the universe wasn't finished with us. It threw us together once again on a blind date, hoping we'd get it right this second time. And just when I thought our paths wouldn't cross again, he showed up at my condo to fix a water leak. And that's when the magic happened, and we got it right on the third try.

This experience taught me a valuable lesson: love has a knack for popping up in the most unexpected moments of our lives. You can't go actively hunting for it, no sirree. Genuine love has a way of finding you when you least expect it. So, keep your heart open and let destiny do its thing. Who knows? Your true love might be just around the next corner, waiting for the right moment to sweep you off your feet.

CHAPTER 28

Christmas Day
my condo

After Griff and I unexpectedly met in my bedroom, we started dating. It brought immense joy to everyone around us. Joshua and Dexter were over the moon with excitement. Finally, I found my special someone. My pinkie ring was back on my finger, and I'll not spend Christmas alone. I guess *alone* isn't the correct word, considering I've got Josh and Dexter. You get what I'm saying? Right?

Christmas Day was absolutely incredible—perfect, like a Hallmark movie. Joshua and Dexter were practically bouncing off the walls, like a couple of excited little kids, as they tore into their presents with pure joy. The living room was an absolute disaster zone, covered in shreds of wrapping paper and colored ribbons. But honestly, who cares? It was Christmas Day, and I couldn't have asked for a better holiday, surrounded by my new boyfriend, Griff, and my two boys, Joshua and Dexter—my chosen family.

We stuffed ourselves with a scrumptious holiday lunch consisting of honey-glazed ham, cranberries, crescent rolls, green beans, and all the classic holiday dishes. And for the grand finale, we pampered ourselves with fruit cake smothered with generous dollops of whipped cream.

After lunch, we gathered around the fireplace. Griff started the fire, and I adjusted the air conditioning to set a winter atmosphere. Despite the lack of snow or chilly weather outside, we refused to let that dampen our spirits. We cozied up to the crackling fire, savoring hot cocoa and indulging in buttery popcorn while enjoying the timeless Christmas movie *It's a*

Wonderful Life on television. It, indeed, was the ideal way to wrap up the holiday.

Imagine this: you're on a carousel, riding on a beautifully painted pony. As you enjoy the ride, you catch a glimpse of something glittering in the distance—a shiny brass ring. That ring symbolizes the ultimate prize, the pinnacle of fulfillment and joy. It's the same in life, isn't it? We're always striving for something special, that moment of pure bliss—reaching for that sparkling brass ring.

But here's the twist—the carousel pony doesn't move in a straight line. Oh no, it goes round and round and up and down, taking you on a ride. Similarly, love takes us on a roller coaster of emotions, highs and lows, twists and turns. It's a ride like none other, but one we willingly embark upon, knowing that the journey is worth the experience.

* * *

Dale Thele

PART TWO

WEDDING WOES

Dale Thele

Tuesday, May 10, 1983

*"We are all a little weird and life's a little weird.
And when we find someone whose weirdness is
compatible with ours, we join up with them
and fall in mutual weirdness and call it love."*

~ Dr. Seuss ~

The year is 1983. Ronald Reagan is running the show as the President of the USA. It's a year of highs and lows, with Hurricane Alicia wreaking havoc on the Texas coast, sadly taking the lives of 22 people and causing a whopping $3.8 billion in damages. On a lighter note, if you need to fill up your car, you'll shell out $1.24 for a gallon of gas.

In the entertainment world, Mario and Luigi, the dynamic duo from the Mario Brothers, burst onto the scene with their video game debut in Japan. Meanwhile, Sally Ride made history as the first American woman to venture into outer space, proving that the sky is no longer the limit for women. And speaking of out-of-this-world experiences, *Star Wars: Return of the Jedi* dominates the box office, captivating audiences with epic battles between good and evil.

Fashion-wise, shoulder pads and cinching belts are all the rage for women, giving them that powerful and confident look. But it's not just fashion that's making waves. Cabbage Patch Kids takes the toy world by storm, becoming the must-have item for kids everywhere. And let's not forget about the King of Pop, Michael Jackson, who dropped his *Thriller* album, forever cementing his place in music history.

Now, let's talk about food. The invention of the Chicken McNugget sends demand for chicken skyrocketing, as people

131

can't resist the crispy and delicious bite-sized pieces of poultry. And finally, we can't overlook the small screen, where the *M*A*S*H* finale captivated audiences and became the most-watched TV show of all time, bidding farewell to beloved characters and leaving a lasting impact on viewers.

Wow, can you believe how quickly time passes? It seems like just yesterday I was in high school, raising cane with my best bud Cal and putting up with ol' man Gardner's crap. But man, that was a whopping nine years ago. Putting it in those terms it seems like an eternity, but when you think about it, it was just a tiny fraction of my life.

Dexter and Joshua are in their second year at the University of Texas, right here in town. They divide their time equally into three parts:

- Going to classes
- Devouring all my food
- Sleeping at their apartment

It's like a never-ending cycle—attending classes, eating and sleeping.

Don't get me wrong, I adore having the boys over. I would genuinely miss them if they stopped coming. However, there are moments when I really crave some alone time. Unfortunately, that seems like a luxury I can only afford on rare occasions. I guess that's just part of the deal when you have kids—or, in my case—when you're an adopted uncle to two teenage boys.

Honestly, I can't deny how much I love having these boys around. They bring me so much joy that I can't imagine life without them. But hey, let's be real here: sometimes I need a break. A little slice of solitude to recharge my batteries. Sadly, those moments are as rare as a Loch Ness Nessie sighting.

You see, being an adopted uncle to two teenage boys comes with unique challenges. It's a constant whirlwind of activity, laughter, and occasional chaos.

A few months back, I'd have weekend mornings to myself,

but lately, even those pockets of me-time are rare and far between. Like I said, I wouldn't trade my time with the boys for the world, but a guy needs a little personal time occasionally, you know?

Imagine having a secret hideout where you can escape the noise and demands of the world. A place where you can be alone with your thoughts, even if it's just for a little while. That's the luxury I yearn for, but it's as elusive as finding a needle in a haystack. But hey, that's the price you pay when you sign up for the *adult guardian/adopted uncle gig*.

The gig is a package deal that includes endless love, unforgettable memories, and a constant need for patience. So, while I may daydream about occasional alone time, I wouldn't trade time with the boys for anything. They're my family, heart, and source of endless amusement. It's all part of the adventure of being an adopted uncle to two incredible teenage boys.

Since Griff and I started dating, there's not been much time for just the two of us. But hey, I'm not complaining. The condo is always buzzing with people and activity. It's like an around-the-clock party. Finding a few moments to spend with Griff amid all this mayhem is a real challenge. You could say I'm selfish, wanting my cake and eating it too. But a little romance time wouldn't hurt a blossoming relationship. Right?

Adding to all the craziness, Griff practically lives here with me, although he hasn't officially moved in yet. Honestly, he might as well; he's almost residing here. It would be good for our relationship if he made it official and moved in. You know what they say, either fish or cut bait. Having him around is great, and our relationship has really taken off. We're doing all those cutesy couple things, like finishing each other's sentences and wearing matching clothes. It's like we're two peas in a pod. Of course, each of us has lives outside of the condo. Let's be real; we have daytime jobs. That's the only time we're apart from each other. And to think all of this came about because I said *yes* when Griff asked me to be his life partner. What more could I ask for, you know? Life's just about as fabulous as it could possibly be.

Griff has settled comfortably into our little tribe. Dexter and Joshua have also accepted him as part of our unconventional family. I have no idea what Griff initially thought before joining a family with two almost-grown boys. Still, he has adapted just fine. We're like one big happy family—Griff, Dexter, Joshua, and me.

It's crazy how families work, you know? Some are naturally related, some are blended with stepparents and stepkids, and some share no natural or legal ties whatsoever. But they're still happy and content. A family is whatever folks make it to be. Personally, I wouldn't trade my *family* for anything in the world. I love them like we're a proper family—because, in my eyes, we are a proper family, maybe even more so. You know what I'm getting at?

CHAPTER 1

Tuesday evening, May 10
my condo

"So, what are you boys planning for your vacation since you're not taking summer classes?" I ask.

"Oh, you know, probably just chill and relax," Dexter replies.

"Can't blame you guys," Griff says. "You've been going to classes continually since graduating high school. You took college classes during the summer semester and then loaded up on courses during the fall and spring semesters. You boys deserve a summer break from the books."

"Yeah, that's exactly what I was thinking, too," Joshua nods.

"Hey, Josh, maybe you could visit your dad," I suggest.

"Yeah, I'd like that," Joshua says.

"Hey, maybe I could come with," Dexter chimes in. "It would be cool to see your ol' man again. We could make a whole day of it."

"Yeah, that sounds like a plan," Joshua nods.

And just like that, the conversation flows effortlessly. It's a typical evening at the condo, with everyone engaged in lively discussions. Several conversations merge while serving bowls of food crisscross the table. Supper at Casa Davison is always filled with energy and noise.

However, amidst all the chatter, I notice Dexter is unusually quiet, appearing lost in thought.

"Dex, you're awfully quiet. Is everything alright?" I ask.

"Yeah, I'm good," he replies, not sharing his thoughts.

"If you want to talk, just know I'm here for you," I assure him.

"Uncle Shane, can I ask you something?" Dexter says.

"Of course, what's on your mind?" I respond, making sure to convey my genuine interest.

"Well, in my ethics class last week," Dexter begins, "we had a discussion that's been bothering me."

"What's bothering you?" I ask, leaning in closer to show my interest.

"My professor brought up the topic of conversion therapy..."

"What's *conversion therapy*?" Joshua blurts.

"Well," Dexter takes a moment to gather his thoughts before continuing, "conversion therapy is a misguided notion that homosexuality is wrong and can be fixed through various methods."

"You see, Josh," I interject. "The concept of conversion therapy is based on an unrealistic theory that a person's homosexual or bisexual orientation can be permanently altered to a heterosexual state."

"Wait," Joshua says, "I don't understand. Explain this to me."

Pausing momentarily, I take a deep breath, mentally preparing to tackle this issue.

"You see," I say, there are people who believe being gay or bi is a learned behavior. And they think that conversion therapy can permanently *fix* the individual into being straight."

"Wait, you mean like a disease?" Joshua interrupts.

I nod.

"Yeah, unfortunately," Griff chimes in, shaking his head. "But the reality is, there's absolutely no solid scientific evidence to support such outrageous ideas."

"So?" Joshua asks. "Where did this conversion therapy thing come from?"

"Well, it started with ultra-conservative Christians who were convinced that being gay or bi isn't only a sin but also goes against the natural order of God's plan," I say.

"That's just plain crazy," Joshua says. "Being gay or bi isn't a sin. At least, I don't think it is. I'm no expert on what the Bible says. But if someone is born gay, like Dex, then it can't be wrong or a sin. It's just the way they naturally are."

"I totally agree," Dexter chimes in. "But not everyone sees it that way. It was crazy how our class was literally split down the middle. Half of the class actually supported the idea of conversion therapy, thinking that being gay can be cured. Can you believe that?"

Joshua shakes his head, his face displaying disbelief.

"It's mind-boggling," Dexter says. "But the other half of the class, they got it right. They understood that being gay isn't some illness that needs fixing. It's simply a natural part of who some people are. You know?"

"Dex, you hit the nail on the head," Joshua says. "Being gay is not a disease; it's just a fundamental aspect of someone's identity. Like that old saying, *a leopard can't change its spots*. No matter how hard you try, you can't alter something inherent to your being. I've never considered Dex to be diseased, and he certainly doesn't need changing."

"Thanks, Josh," Dexter says.

"Besides, you can't help that you're not as good-looking as me," Joshua teases.

"Alright," Dexter interrupts, "that's enough out of you. Besides, who says it's not you breeders who need fixing?"

"Okay, boys," I step in before World War III breaks out at my dining table.

"I'm afraid we're going to hear a lot more about this in the coming years as the discussion of conversion therapy becomes more prevalent," Griff says, shaking his head.

"Dex," I interrupt. "We kind of got sidetracked. What was your question about conversion therapy?"

"Well," Dexter says. "What do you know about how it works? Do you know anyone who's been through it?"

"Yeah, I guess I do," I reply.

"Can you tell me about it?" Dexter asks.

"I was in the middle of my freshman year in college," I say. "When I came face-to-face with my dorm suite-mate. It's funny because we managed to go through the entire first semester without even bumping into each other. We shared a single bathroom between our two rooms. But this guy was like some sort of phantom, always keeping to himself and being super quiet.

"Anyway, I was brushing my teeth in our adjoining bathroom one evening when he accidentally walked in. When he saw me, he freaked out and retreated into his room, locking the door behind him. I wrapped up my teeth-brushing session and informed him that the bathroom was available, mentioning that I was heading back to my room.

"A few days later, we bumped into each other in the hall outside our rooms. I introduced myself, and he introduced himself as Russel. From then on, we started hanging out now and then. As the semester went on, I found out some stuff about Russel. He was from Illinois and had a messed up relationship with his dad—a Church of Christ preacher in a small one-church town. He told me this heartbreaking story about how his dad caught him kissing another boy when he was in junior high. As punishment, Russel's dad sent Russel to a church-sponsored conversion therapy center a couple of hundred miles away.

"While at the center, he was physically abused, humiliated, and even starved. Russel said they kept him drugged to the point that he couldn't comprehend what was happening to him. In rare moments of clarity, he realized the only way out of the conversion therapy center was to pretend he was *cured*.

"After six long months, he was released to his parents. That's when he truly realized how cruel some *church going people* can be. The whole experience messed him up so badly that he swore he'd do anything to avoid going back. Russel also told me about the other boys in that place going through the similar bullshit. None of them were getting *fixed* of their homosexuality. Instead, the beatings and starvation just made them angry. Russel knew when he returned home, he couldn't stay because he feared losing control and going off on his dad. So, he left home and went to live with his accepting grandma. Eventually, he scored a full scholarship to Oklahoma City University, where I had the honor of meeting Russel."

The dining room suddenly becomes quiet, enveloping us in complete silence.

"Wow! What a story," Dexter exclaims. "I wish that Russel guy had spoken to my class. He would've left a lasting impression."

Silent contemplation overtakes the room.

"Here's something I've never told anyone," I say, breaking the silence. "When I was about twelve, I was close to being sent to conversion camp."

"What?!" Dexter's jaw drops in disbelief.

"It was the start of summer break when I wasn't certain if maybe I might be sent away. School had just ended until the fall term, and I was starting my three-month summer vacation from school. When, out of the blue, a bunch of ladies from church showed up at our house. I remember Momma answering the door while I watched from the hall. Momma invited the ladies inside, and they settled in the living room.

"Then, out of nowhere, one of the ladies brought up *conversion therapy camp* and told my Momma to send me there. Momma didn't say a word.

But the other ladies jumped in, and before I knew it, they were practically screaming at Momma, trying to convince her that conversion camp was some kind of miracle solution for me.

I wanted to storm into the living room and defend Momma from those crazy church ladies, but I couldn't risk her finding out I was eavesdropping. She caught me once. I got in big trouble, and she threatened me, *If I ever catch you listening in on my private conversations, I'll—I'll—*. She never finished the threat, but I knew she wasn't joking.

"Anyway, Momma didn't say a word to those ladies, either for or against the idea. Eventually, those ladies gave up and left, probably realizing they weren't getting anywhere with Momma.

"Back then, I'd never heard of conversion camp or what it meant to be homosexual. It was another four years before I learned its meaning and another year before I came out as gay.

So there I was, utterly confused and clueless about what those ladies were blabbering on about.

It was a rough time for both Momma and me. Momma and Daddy were getting a divorce, and I didn't know anyone my age whose parents were divorced, so everything was confusing and new to me. Since I had no one to confide in, I had to figure things out on my own.

I reckon Momma was in the same boat. She did her darnedest to navigate the choppy waters of divorce while keeping her cool."

"So, what happened?" Joshua asks.

"Not much," I say. "Momma never mentioned that day or why those ladies were so upset."

"Looking back," Griff asks, "what do you think was going through your mom's mind?"

"Honestly, Momma was overwhelmed with the whole divorce thing. She had much more pressing matters to attend to than concerning herself with the opinions of those nosy church women. She was a truly independent thinker and always followed her own moral compass. I got to say, I was incredibly proud of Momma for standing up for herself and not allowing those self-righteous church biddies to dictate how she should raise her kid. Had she caved, I have no idea what kind of person I'd have become or if I would be here today."

"Wow," Dexter exclaims, his eyes widen in surprise. "Why have you never told us this story before?"

I take a deep breath, contemplating how to respond.

"Well, it happened a long time ago," I say. "Honestly, it's not something I feel comfortable discussing. That's why I've never brought it up."

"But seriously," Joshua interjects, "you could have been sent off to a conversion camp?"

"To be completely honest, I don't believe so," I confess. "You see, whenever I misbehaved, Momma threatened to ship me off to military school. However, deep down, I knew her threats were just that—threats. Our financial struggles made it clear that she simply couldn't afford to send me away, whether it was to a military school or some conversion camp."

"Finances aside," Griff says, "do you think there might have been another factor at play that influenced her choice not to send you to camp?"

"Well," I pause momentarily, then continue. "There might have been another reason. It may have had something to do with Momma's cousin."

"What's this about a cousin?" Griff asks.

"I don't have all the specifics," I say, "but from what I recall, I began connecting the dots as I grew older. Of course, I may have misinterpreted the situation, but I genuinely don't believe I did."

"What exactly are you trying to say?" Dexter asks.

"Alright, let me start over," I say. "Momma had this cousin. He was younger than her, maybe by eight or ten years. Everyone called him Jimmie except for his mom—Momma's aunt. She called him *James*. Jimmie lived with my aunt in a small town in Kansas, pretty close to the northern border of Oklahoma. We didn't visit them too often, but I can still picture their place in my mind. It was out in the country—in the middle of nowhere. Her place was a one-story, brick, ranch-style house. The bricks were light blond, and the roof was all sun-bleached, almost matching the color of the bricks. If you looked for the house from a distance, you could hardly tell the house apart from the sun-scorched trees and tall dead grass surrounding it.

"I remember our visits to Aunt Hilda's house. Jimmie entered the living room shortly after we'd arrive. He always entertained us kids with the funniest stories. Spending time with Jimmie was a blast. After a while, Aunt Hilda abruptly interrupted and instructed Jimmie to take his medicine. He'd excuse himself and retreat to his bedroom, where he'd nap. Us kids wouldn't see Jimmie any further during that visit.

There was something about Jimmie that the adults wouldn't talk about. You see, Jimmie wasn't allowed to be alone with us kids—not without adult supervision. I couldn't understand why;

after all, he was an adult. So, I went to Momma for answers, but she brushed me off, saying *it's none of your business*. That got me thinking: *why was Jimmie not allowed to be around kids without supervision?* Clearly, he loved being with us kids, and we liked being around him, too."

"Even as a kid, I sensed something off about Jimmie. It wouldn't be until years later that I began to understand the situation surrounding Cousin Jimmie."

"So, what was going on with Jimmie?" An intrigued Joshua inquires.

"Sorry for interrupting," Griff says, "but it seems to me that Jimmie may have been a child molester. Of course, I don't have all the details, but from what you've said, it's possible that a judge showed leniency and made Jimmie your Aunt Hilda's ward. That's not uncommon in small rural communities."

"That's what I thought," I say, nodding in agreement.

"How did your mom react when you discovered Jimmy's true nature?" Josh asks.

"We never talked about stuff like that," I confess.

"You must've had a really sheltered childhood," Griff comments.

"Yeah, it was," I reply. "I had to figure things out on my own because neither Momma nor Daddy discussed what they called *uncomfortable subjects*. It wasn't until I was older that I realized I'd been raised in an overly protective environment. Until then, I didn't think anything was amiss; I assumed we were like any other family.

However, as I grew older, my perspective shifted. I figured out I'd been overly protected all my childhood. I lived in a safety bubble, shielded from the bad things of the real world."

"Did that piss you off that they did that to you?" Dexter asks.

"Yeah, it did. I never forgave them for treating me like that," I confess. "But looking back, I realize my parents had good intentions. It was a different time, and people did things differently then. They just wanted to keep me safe and protected from potential harm. Unfortunately, their over-protectiveness had unintended consequences. It prevented me from fully experiencing life, learning essential life lessons, and developing proper social skills.

In my innocence, I assumed we were like any other family. I had no point of reference to compare my upbringing with others. I would be older when I realized how sheltered my life had been when I stepped out into the real world and interacted with people from different backgrounds.

As an adult, I strive to balance caution and exploration. I understand the importance of protecting oneself, but I also see the value in taking risks and embracing new experiences. Through these experiences, we grow, learn, and better understand the world around us.

The room falls silent. I can't tell what Joshua, Dexter, and Griff are thinking. Maybe they're pondering what I just revealed about my childhood, or perhaps they feel sorry for me and my unconventional upbringing. Whatever the reason, the silence makes me uncomfortable. I'm accustomed to rowdy and rambunctious teenage boys being adolescent boys.

Dale Thele

CHAPTER 2

Wednesday evening, May 11
my condo

I glance at Griff, who's sitting across the table. He gives a gentle nod before clearing his throat. I know what he's about to say—we discussed it earlier, unsure of how the boys might react to the bomb we are about to drop on them. Griff nudges me with his eyes, silently urging me to get on with it. It seems he's chickened out and is leaving it up to me to break the news.

"Uh, boys," I say, trying to prolong this conversation for as long as possible. I've played this scenario in my mind countless times, imagining all sorts of different reactions. Honestly, I have no clue how they'll respond to what I'm about to reveal.

"Alright, boys," I say, gathering my thoughts and searching for the right words.

"What's on your mind?" Dexter breaks in with a concerned expression.

"Just say it already," Joshua interrupts, "if you have something on your mind, spit it out."

"Well..." I pause, mentally searching for the perfect words to express myself. "I'm trying to find the right way to put this."

"It can't be that bad, can it? Or is it?" Dexter asks.

"You're making me nervous, Uncle Shane," Joshua says.

"No, it's nothing bad, I promise. Well, at least I hope you won't perceive it as bad," I say to the boys.

"Come on," Dexter urges, "Uncle Shane, tell us already! I'm dying to know."

"Shane, you'd best get on with it," Griff nods, encouraging me to continue. "Go on."

"Alright," I say, picking up a glass of water and taking a sip as a stall tactic. "You know Griff and I've become really close."

"No kidding," Joshua replies.

"Well, Griff asked me to—" I'm abruptly interrupted.

"Griff proposed, and you're planning a commitment ceremony?" Dexter exclaims, practically jumping out of his chair with excitement.

"How did you come to that conclusion?" I ask Dexter.

"Easy," Dexter says, grinning. "That's the next logical step in your relationship."

"I don't get it," Joshua says, scratching his head in confusion. "What the heck is a *commitment ceremony*?"

"It's like a wedding," Dexter explains.

"Then why not call it a wedding?" Joshua asks.

"Because legally, gays and lesbians can't get married," Dexter clarifies.

"Oh," Joshua responds, surprised. "I didn't know that."

"A commitment ceremony," Dexter excitedly explains to Joshua, "is essentially the closest that same-sex couples have to a traditional wedding."

"So," Joshua asks, "what exactly happens during a commitment ceremony?"

"Well," Griff smiles and explains, "a commitment ceremony is a celebration of love and dedication between two individuals. It's a way for a couple to publicly declare their unwavering commitment to each other without the legal formalities of a traditional wedding. Think of it as a personalized and intimate gathering where the couple can express their unique love story."

"Josh," I say, leaning in close to emphasize the significance of our discussion, "the event we're planning is like a wedding. Instead of exchanging vows, Griff and I will publicly express our love for each other in front of our loved ones and friends."

"That sounds pretty cool," Joshua's eyes sparkle with growing interest.

"So, can Josh and I be part of this ceremony?" Dexter asks.

"Well, Griff and I hoped you boys would want to be a part of it. You boys are family. However, I must ask something important before we get ahead of ourselves. Josh, are you okay with Griff and me having this commitment ceremony?"

"Why are you asking me?" Joshua asks.

"Well," I say, "your dad and I, you know, were together, and..."

"Stop right there," Joshua interrupts. "I'm cool with you and Griff doing this. Besides, how often has Dad told you he wants you to move on? He doesn't expect you to wait forever for him to, you know, get out of prison."

"I just want you to be okay with this," I explain. "I don't want you to think I'm disrespecting your dad or anything."

"I'm happy for you, really," Joshua reassures me. "You and Griff should tie the knot."

"It's not really a marriage," I clarify.

"I get it," Joshua replies. "You're talking about a commitment ceremony." Grinning, he playfully makes air quote gestures around *commitment ceremony*.

"When are you planning to do this?" Dexter asks.

"Well," Griff replies, "we were thinking in two weeks."

"Two weeks?" Dexter jumps up from his chair. "That's not nearly enough time to organize such an important event. There are invitations to be sent, booking a venue, ordering the flowers..."

"And hey, let's not forget ordering the cake," Joshua pipes up.

"Seriously, two weeks won't cut it," Dexter crosses his arms over his chest.

"Hold up, you guys," I say. "We don't want anything fancy or showy. Okay?"

"Just a small gathering of our close friends and family," Griff adds.

"But, Uncle Shane," Dexter jumps in. "This is a major milestone; it should be grand and fabulous!"

"Alright, listen up," I explain. "Griff knows this couple who's offered to host a simple, intimate event in their backyard flower garden. It has a pond with Koi, surrounded by Weeping

Willows, a water fountain, and lots of blooming flowers. It's a small and elegant setting."

"But, Uncle Shane," Dexter protests.

"Dex, hold on a sec," I interrupt. "It's all settled, and most details are already sorted."

"Well, in that case," Dexter retorts, "just for the record, I think you're making a big mistake."

"Duly noted," I say, flashing a grin.

It's a relief to see that I've pretty much convinced the boys that our ceremony will be a small affair, and they seem to be on board with Griff and me doing this.

"So, who will be on the guest list?" Dexter asks.

"Obviously, you boys," I reply, "you're family."

"And I'm inviting my mom," Griff adds.

"That covers all our close relatives," I explain.

"We'll also invite some of our closest friends," Griff grins.

"What about Uncle Cal?" Dexter asks. "Is he getting an invitation, too?"

"No," I shake my head, "Cal has agreed to be my right-hand man."

"Like a best man, huh?" Joshua asks.

"Yeah, something like that," I agree.

"Griff, do you have someone to stand with you?" Joshua asks.

"Absolutely!" Griff replies with a smile. "My best friend from college. I'm sure you'll like him."

"Wow," Dexter exclaims, "it sounds like you've got this under control."

"Well, to some extent," I remark. "We deliberately kept this news under wraps until we were absolutely certain about our decision. Griff initially brought up the idea; surprisingly, everything fell into place."

"I still wish you'd hold off so we can plan a bigger event," Dexter grumbles.

"Come on, Dex, let it go," Joshua retorts. "This is Griff and Uncle Shane's decision, and we should respect their wishes.

After all, it's their wedding."

"Commitment ceremony!" Griff, Dexter, and I correct in unison.

"Semantics, schematics, it's all the same," Joshua dismisses, getting up from the table and carrying his dirty plate to the kitchen.

Well, well, well, isn't this a surprise? I think to myself. I can't recall a single instance when either of the boys has taken the initiative to clear their dirty dishes after a meal—at least not as long as I've known them. I wonder if Joshua's coming down with something?

Dale Thele

CHAPTER 3

Thursday afternoon, May 12
Griff's condo

" 'My only son is not getting married in some random backyard flower garden. Let's reconsider the situation. However, don't you fret. I'll take charge to ensure you have a proper and sophisticated wedding. Believe you me, this wedding will be the talk of the social season, perhaps even the entire year. Be patient; I'll bring you in on the particulars once I've booked the ideal venue.'

"Click.

"Mumsy hung up on me just like that," he says, rolling his eyes. "She didn't even let me get a word in edgewise. Classic, Mumsy." Griff angrily shakes his head. "Man, oh man, I seriously regret inviting her. I should've known she'd hijack the whole shebang."

"I understand that dealing with your mom can be quite challenging sometimes," I say. "However, I'm sure you can convince her to organize a cozy, little, intimate celebration."

"No way," he fumes, shaking his head adamantly. "Once Mumsy gets an idea stuck in her head, there's no changing it. Trust me, I've tried, and it's utterly futile. I'm telling you, it's a lost cause."

"Alright, so how much are we looking at in terms of cost? You know, just a rough estimate," I say, sensing a cold sweat forming on my forehead and visualizing my bank account rapidly dwindling.

"Nothing," Griff says.

His unexpected response catches me entirely off guard.

"What?" I ask, raising a questioning brow.

"Don't worry," Griff chuckles, "this won't cost us a single

penny. Mumsy will take care of all the expenses. She's always generous when impressing her socialite friends."

"If she's footing the bill for a ceremony like you suggest, it's bound to cost her a small fortune. It's wrong for us to expect her to bear the entire financial burden."

"Why not? It's every bit her idea," Griff says.

"But—?" I'm cut off before I can finish my question.

"There's something I haven't been frank with you about, Mumsy. I suppose now is as good as any to tell you."

Narrowing my eyes, I'm skeptical of his tone.

"What are you trying to say? Is there something I should know about your mom? Come on, out with it," I say, closing my eyes and mentally preparing myself for bad news.

"Alright, Shane," Griff says, "but first, you need to sit down."

"I don't like where this is going," I say.

"You're bound to find this out sooner or later," Griff says. "I might as well come clean."

There's a long pause as Griff looks at the floor.

I'm nervously wringing my hands.

"Mumsy is stinking loaded," Griff blurts, like ripping off a band-aid.

"Loaded?" I shoot Griff a puzzled look. "What are you saying—she's a drunken alcoholic?"

"Not quite," Griff chuckles. "Mumsy is loaded, as in she's ridiculously rich."

"WHAT?" I say. "Are you telling me you come from money? I mean, I had no idea. I know you live comfortably and don't seem to hurt for anything. It doesn't matter, but it could have been helpful to have known this earlier."

"Mumsy is none other than Jacqueline Rowling-Sakowitz-Goldman-Barrows, the eccentric Dallas socialite," Griff confesses.

"Wow," I say as the shock wears off. "You're seriously rich."

"No, I'm not rich," Griff corrects me. "Mumsy is the one

with the money. I have no connection to her wealth. I worked for what I have."

"But?" I ask, scratching my head. "I don't get it."

"Mumsy and I had a big falling out a while back—before you and I ever met. I packed my bags and left Dallas. That's when I settled in Austin and started my plumbing business. Let me tell you, the business took off like gangbusters. I was booking appointments with high-end clients left and right. But here's the kicker: it took me a whole year to realize that dear ol' Mumsy was behind those bookings. She was quietly sending me clients. Being a Barrows, I should've known I could never escape her money. Mumsy was all up in my business. I thought I was this amazing businessman, but it was all her doing."

"But you're a good businessman," I say. "You're fair, honest, and a damn good plumber."

"Thanks," Griff says. "But Mumsy initially built my business without me realizing it."

"Does it really matter how you landed your first clients?" I ask. "You've worked hard building your business and earning your reputation."

"Well, the thing is, my reputation is tied to being a Barrows —you know, from the Dallas Barrows," Griff explains.

"Okay, I see your point," I reply. "Can we change the subject? Because I have a question. Tell me, your mom has been married a few times, right? So, how many times? I've heard three and maybe four times. Which is it?"

"Five times, to be precise," Griff confirms.

"Holy crap! THAT many times?" I exclaim, taking a moment to consider what that entails. "Hold on a second. If she's been married so many times, how is it that you have the Barrows' last name?"

"That's because my ol' man was a Barrows'," Griff explains.

"Wait, so was your dad the last guy she married?" I ask.

"Heavens, no," Griff shakes his head. "My father was Mumsy's first husband—"

"That's what I don't get—your mom's last name is

Barrows."

"That's right." Griff says, "Let's start at the beginning. Mumsy's first husband was Hubert Darius Barrows, who was my biological dad. It didn't take long before they divorced. Mumsy then tied the knot with Robert Winston Rowling, but that marriage didn't last either. Next up was Samuel Aviv Elijah Sakowitz, and you guessed it, they ended up divorcing, too. After that, she married Sherman Abraham Goldman, but that marriage dissolved miserably. And finally, she walked down the aisle with Bartholomew Edmonds Barrows III."

"Oh, I see," I say, beginning to understand. "Your mom married two different guys, who were both named Barrows."

"Yup," Griff replies. "Mumsy dropped the first Barrows from her string of last names—that was my biological dad. Then, later on, she married another Barrows. He's actually my dad's second or third cousin. Mumsy added the second *Barrows* to the string of other husbands' last names."

"Do you still keep in touch with your dad?"

"Nah," Griff says. "He and Mumsy split about the time when they sent me to a European private elementary school. Not long after, he passed from a heart attack. I never really got the chance to know him."

"Are you on good terms with your stepdad?" I ask.

"Which one?" Griff chuckles.

"I guess I'm talking about the most recent one?" I inquire, raising an eyebrow.

"You mean my dad's cousin?" he asks.

"Okay? So, what's his deal?" I ask, genuinely confused.

"Mumsy and cousin Barty called it quits just a few months after tying the knot. Barty moved to Australia, and I don't think she's heard from him since."

"Sounds like your mom has had rough luck in the marriage department, huh? No offense." I can't help but chuckle.

"None taken." He shrugs, and a smile breaks across his face. "Let me tell you, Mumsy is what's called a *career bride*."

"What do you mean by that?" I ask.

"She keeps marrying but never commits to being a wife. She marries for the sport and the financial gain."

"So, let me get this straight. Instead of collecting trading stamps, your mom collects husbands?"

"Yeah, but here's the kicker—she's not just any ordinary husband collector. Oh no, she's a pro at marrying wealthy men, getting large sums of cash and bonds, and gaining control of their companies in huge divorce settlements."

"I'm at a loss for words, really, I am."

"Well, there's not much to say, I guess. I've come to terms with the fact that I have a filthy-rich, eccentric mother. It's just the way things are."

"You know, you're making it sound like it's not such a bad thing."

"Hold your judgment until you've met her. Trust me, once you meet the one and only Mrs. Jacqueline Rowling-Sakowitz-Goldman-Barrows, you'll understand why I had to get out of Dallas as fast as possible. She's a force to be reckoned with, that's for sure."

After our chat, Griff contacted his friends, who own the stunning, award-winning backyard flower garden. He politely declined their offer to use the garden for our ceremony, explaining that his mom had different plans. Meanwhile, I called Cal to bring him up to speed on the change of plans. I told him I'd phone him when we had a new date. Griff did the same with his college buddy, Stone.

Now, we wait for Mrs. Rowling-Sakowitz-Goldman-Barrows to make her next move. It's like the intense atmosphere of a chess match. The spectators wait for the opponent to make their next move. The anticipation has everyone on the edge of their seats, wondering what comes next.

Dale Thele

CHAPTER 4

Saturday afternoon, May 21
Griff's condo

Griff and I are returning to my condo after an enjoyable brunch at one of Austin's finer restaurants. On the way, we stop by his place. Griff parks his car in the building garage, and we walk to his condo. Getting off the elevator near his place, we hear his phone ringing.

Griff fumbles with his keys in a panic, attempting to unlock the door in time to answer the call.

Sensing his struggle, I snatch his keys and open the door for him.

Griff rushes inside, answering the call before the caller hangs up.

It doesn't take a rocket scientist to figure out who's on the other end of the call, especially when Griff blurts out an exasperated *Yes, Mumsy* into the receiver.

Trying not to eavesdrop is difficult when Griff's angry voice fills the condo, making it impossible for me to ignore the one-sided conversation. I can imagine what Mrs. Rowling-Sakowitz-Goldman-Barrows is spewing from the other end of the call.

She cuts him off mid-sentence, allowing Griff the occasional grunt, leaving him visibly frustrated. With each passing moment, his face turns redder, a clear sign of his growing frustration.

"Bye, Mumsy," he spits, forcefully slamming the receiver onto the phone base. Running his hands over his face, he's exasperated with his mom.

"That woman drives me absolutely crazy," Griff fumes.

His last comment was more like an internal thought to himself rather than something he intended for me to hear.

"So, how's your mom?" I say, trying to lighten the mood.

Griff shoots me an angry glare, sending a shiver down my spine. Without saying a word, he takes a few deliberate deep breaths before responding.

"Can you believe it?" He says. "Good ol' Mumsy booked the Cornerstone Cathedral Church for our ceremony."

"Oh my gosh!" I exclaim. "That's the largest church in all of Central Texas. What? Wasn't the Vatican available?"

"Seriously, don't even go there," Griff snips, anger written on his face. "I mean, come on, knowing her, she most likely started with the Vatican and worked her way down the list of largest to smallest venues."

I don't want to risk getting my head bitten off, so I nod and keep my mouth shut.

"By the way, block out Saturday, August 6, on your calendar," he says. "That's the day she reserved the Cathedral." Griff falls silent for a moment, then his expression softens as he looks at me and says, "Babe, I'm really sorry. I didn't even ask if that date works for you."

"It's probably okay," I say, mentally running through the list of my upcoming appointments.

He gives me another one of those deadly glares.

"Um," I stutter, realizing that Griff's in no joking mood. "Now that I think about it, I'm pretty sure I'm free that day."

Snapping his neck, he shoots me a piercing, squint-eyed glare.

"You know what?" I say. "On second thought, I know for a fact. I'm free on that day," I say with an approving nod.

I'm realizing that you don't mess with Mrs. Jacqueline Rowling-Sakowitz-Goldman-Barrows. You do what she says, or else. And honestly, I'm not brave enough to find out what *or else* might entail. Griff's glares give me a glimpse of the unpleasantness that awaits those who dare to challenge Mumsy. I've made up my mind not to question Mrs. Rowling-Sakowitz-Goldman-Barrows. Her word is law, and I'll comply without hesitation, even if her son relays it to me.

"Oh, and you won't believe what else she did. My dear Mumsy hired the one and only Wedding Planner to the Stars—Garreth Von Cartier." Griff paces back and forth, seething with anger, desperately trying to keep his fury in check as he mutters incomprehensible phrases through gritted teeth.

"Isn't that the guy from that TV show who organizes fancy celebrity weddings?" I ask.

"Yeah, that's the one, alright," Griff grumbles, clearly ticked off. "You and I are meeting with him next week."

"Will your mom be there?" I inquire, feeling my parched throat as I attempt to swallow.

"Nah," Griff shakes his head. "Thank God for small favors."

An intense silence blankets the room. I'm relieved that Mrs. Rowling-Sakowitz-Goldman-Barrows won't attend the planning meeting. However, it's unsettling to see Griff so angry. I know his anger isn't directed at me; it's aimed at his mom. She knows exactly how to push his buttons to get under his skin. I haven't had the chance to meet my future mother-in-law yet, not that our commitment ceremony will make Mrs. Rowling-Sakowitz-Goldman-Barrows a legal relative. But a part of me is curious to meet her, while another part wonders if it's even worth it. You know what I'm saying?

"There's something else," Griff confesses. "Mumsy wants a photo of you and me for the newspaper wedding announcement."

I raise an eyebrow, trying to grasp his words.

"Does your mother realize this is not a traditional wedding but a GAY commitment ceremony?"

"Not exactly..." he trails off, looking away from me.

Griff's response does little to ease my worries. I feel a sense of unease creeping up on me, urging me to dig deeper.

"Why do I feel that you're hiding something from me? What are you keeping to yourself?"

Griff falls silent and takes a deep breath, avoiding eye contact. There's a moment of hesitation before he finally speaks, his voice barely audible.

"Mumsy has no idea that I'm... well... gay," he says.

"What?" I say, my jaw drops in disbelief. "Are you telling me that you haven't come out to your mom?"

His shoulders slump, and he sinks into a chair, his body language reflecting the inner turmoil he's experiencing.

"The timing has never been right," he confesses, his voice filled with regret.

"Griff, you must tell her and do it soon. Otherwise, she'll find out at our ceremony—the very event she's paying for."

"I understand," he says. "I promise I'll tell her. You have my word."

"Griff, I expect you to keep that promise."

He responds in a barely audible, "I promise."

Silence overtakes the room again.

"I truly hope I can," Griff mumbles under his breath.

"Did you say something?" I ask.

"No," Griff quickly denies. "I didn't say anything."

I'm not imagining things. I distinctly heard him. It's just the two of us in the room, and no matter how much he denies it, I heard him loud and clear. It does worry me that he said, *I hope I can.* You know what I mean?

CHAPTER 5

Thursday late afternoon, May 31
Savoy Hotel restaurant

Griff and I have our first scheduled meeting with Mr. Garreth Von Cartier at the Savoy Hotel restaurant. We arrive early, wanting to make a good impression. But let me tell you, Mr. Von Cartier makes quite an impressive entrance by showing up fashionably late. He strolls into the restaurant with exaggerated arm gestures and wrists flapping, followed by a timid group of staffing assistants. The entourage resembles a mini gay pride parade, minus the marching band.

"I don't have the time right now," Von Cartier says to no one in particular in a dismissive tone. "Pencil her in for a week from Thursday."

It's as if Griff and I catch him wrapping up important business as he arrives for our meeting.

The dutiful assistants scribble notations in their sleek, black leather notebooks, moving like a well-oiled machine in perfect unison.

"Who's next?" Von Cartier asks no one in particular. He throws it out into the air, like a ball, expecting an assistant to catch it and run with it.

Instead, the attendants turn to each other with questioning expressions.

"Well?" Von Cartier asks in a harsh, demanding tone.

The small crowd of conservatively dressed staffers step back one step, leaving a young staffer standing all alone. It is as if she didn't receive the memo that she will be the group's designated spokesperson.

She's nicely dressed in a navy skirt and blazer combination, which exudes professionalism. At the same time, her crisp white blouse, buttoned up to the neck, adds a touch of modesty. A slim navy satin ribbon adorns her high collar, meticulously tied into a dainty bow.

"The next appointment is with a certain Mr. Barrows of the Dallas Barrows," the solo staff member timidly announces.

"What is the first name of Mr. Barrow's fiancée?" Von Cartier asks, his voice tinged with boredom.

The solo staffer turns to the other staffers and shrugs.

The staffers hurriedly shuffle through their papers and notebooks, desperately searching for the answer.

"Sir, it's Shannon," a male staffer responds, his voice brimming with relief. "Her name is Shannon, sir."

"And what pray-tell is Miss Shannon's last name?" asks a frustrated Von Cartier, raising his voice.

"I'm awfully sorry, sir, I don't have that information," the male staffer shrinks and bows as if answering to the Queen of England.

Annoyed, Von Cartier gestures wildly as if testing the air before taking flight. "Does anyone know the fiancée's last name?"

The room echoes with rustling papers as the staffers frantically flip through their notes.

"Never mind," Mr. Von Cartier says with a dramatic wave of his hand.

The gaggle of staffers retreat into the shadows to tend to their wounded egos.

Honestly, the whole scene is funny as hell. Von Cartier's flashy entrance and carefree attitude make it hard to envision him as a competent wedding planner.

Suddenly, Mr. Von Cartier raises his arm and snaps his fingers.

"Sir," says an enthusiastic restaurant server rushing to his side. "Mr. Von Cartier, please allow me to show you to your table, sir."

Wait, did the server actually bow to Von Cartier? It's truly unbelievable. Has everyone gone completely bonkers over this

TV celebrity wedding planner?

Anyway, the two of them take a few steps forward, and the server points to the table in front of Von Cartier. The same table where Griff and I are sitting.

"Ah, Mr. Barrows, I presume?" Von Cartier asks, his eyes darting back and forth between Griff and me. It's as if Von Cartier's eyes are following a ball during a tennis match.

"Griffen Barrows, that's me," Griff responds, half-raising his arm like a shy schoolchild in a classroom.

"Of course you are," Von Cartier remarks, eyeing Griff up and down. He then shoots me a look of disapproval and condescension. Rolling his eyes, Von Cartier makes me feel unworthy to be in his holiness's presence.

In my head, I say, *Fuck You,* to the pompous wedding planner while forcing an exaggerated fake smile.

Griff extends his hand to Mr. Von Cartier, who reluctantly reciprocates with a feeble handshake. Griff then gestures towards me.

"This is Shane Davison," Griff introduces me.

"Pleasure to meet you," Von Cartier halfheartedly says to me as he scans the room, searching for something while he settles into a chair at the table.

"Mr. Von Cartier, is there a problem?" Griff asks.

"Where's your fiancée, Shannon, or whatever her name is?" Von Cartier asks, sounding confused and bored.

"Well, there's been a little mix-up. You see, Shane is my partner, and you've been hired to..."

"Organize a fabulous wedding for Griffen Barrows and his fiancée Shannon, or whatever her name is," Von Cartier chimes in, completing Griff's sentence.

"Not exactly," Griff clarifies. "You see, there isn't a Shannon."

Von Cartier suddenly freezes, looking like a mesmerizing ice sculpture with wide, startled eyes of a caught fish.

The air is thick with apprehension as nervous glances are exchanged.

"Mr. Griffen," Von Cartier says, "I must meet with you and your fair fiancé to go over the details of your big day. Mrs. Jacqueline Rowling-Sakowitz-Goldman-Barrows has requested this meeting, so where may I find Miss Shannon?" He turns and says to me, "Please don't take offense, sir, whoever you are." His laser gaze doesn't waver off me. "Go away," he shoos at me like I'm some filthy farm chicken.

"Um, excuse me, Mr. Von Cart-e-aye—" Griff pipes up, his voice cracking like a pubescent teenage boy.

Von Cartier shudders as if he's swallowed something genuinely repulsive and jumps to his feet.

"The name is pronounced Von Cart-ee-AIR," Von Cartier corrects in a snooty tone.

"Mr. Von Cart-ee-AIR," Griff repeats, putting the emphasis on the last syllable. "Mrs. Rowling-Sakowitz-Goldman-Barrows happens to be my mother, and it seems there's a minor issue with this arrangement."

"And what might this issue be exactly?" Mr. Von Cartier asks, with annoyance in his voice.

"Well, you see, Mr. Von Cartier," Griff begins, "my mother is completely unaware of my orientation. I haven't come out to her yet," Griff confesses to Mr. Von Cartier.

Von Cartier's face turns an alarming shade of pale.

"Sir?" Von Cartier asks. "Are you telling me that *you* are homosexual? And that your mother is unaware of this itsy-bitsy crumb of information?" Von Cartier says. "As for the wedding? Is there to be a wedding? And who exactly is to be wed?"

"My boyfriend Shane and I want a commitment ceremony," Griff says. "But Mumsy can't know it's not a traditional wedding—at least not till I come out to her."

Von Cartier wobbles as if he might collapse at any moment.

Griff and I swiftly react, guiding Mr. Von Cartier to a nearby chair to ensure he has a safe landing.

As I fan him with a menu, Griff requests water from a server to assist our flustered guest—only designer bottled water—of course.

Let me tell you our first meeting with Mr. Von Cartier was a total disaster right from the get-go. Things eventually turned around, and we had a half-decent early supper. As we dined, Mr. Von Cartier agreed to keep Griff's gay secret under wraps until Griff comes out to his mom. Meanwhile, Mr. Von Cartier promised to keep Griff's mom in the loop about the progress of the wedding preparations he's organizing. Little does Mrs. Jacqueline Rowling-Sakowitz-Goldman-Barrows know Von Cartier is secretly organizing a fabulous gay commitment ceremony for Griff and me.

With Griff and my private details sorted with Von Cartier, there's absolutely no way anything could possibly go wrong. Am I right?

CHAPTER 6

Saturday morning, June 4
my condo

At precisely 9:15 am, a sleek limousine glides to a stop at the curb outside my condo to whisk Griff and me away. Anxious, we hop into the opulent white stretch limo to be greeted by Mr. Von Cartier, exuding an air of utmost relaxation with his legs crossed. In one hand, he holds a crystal flute brimming with a tantalizing mimosa. In contrast, the other hand wildly dances in the air. It's as if his mouth cannot function without the accompaniment of his animated gestures, his hands and arms flailing about with great fervor.

Today will be a crazy day as we tackle necessary errands leading up to our big commitment ceremony. Our first stop is to sample and select entrées for the reception dinner. Griff and I aren't exactly fancy eaters. Griff is all about bloody red meat and baked potatoes, while I'm perfectly content with good ol' crispy fried chicken. But Mr. Von Cartier has different ideas. So, after sampling a smorgasbord of foods I can't pronounce, we end up with Grass-fed Angus Filet Mignon and Bresse chicken. Griff is getting his red meat fix, and I'm getting what is supposed to be chicken, but it doesn't taste like any chicken I've ever had. Mr. Von Cartier and the chef pair each entrée with fancy vegetable sides, again with names I can't pronounce. Without even asking us, Mr. Von Cartier sets the menu. He acts like Griff, and I can't make our own choices and slaps his seal of approval on everything *he* wants.

Our next destination is the bakery, where we enjoy a delectable array of sample cakes for our *wedding* cake. Griff is obsessed with rich chocolate cake, while I'm in the mood for a timeless classic—white cake. I wouldn't mind a middle ground with a half-and-half or a checkerboard cake. However, Mr. Von Cartier remains as stubborn as ever, disregarding our preferences. He insists on a Lemon Champagne Cake adorned with heavenly white icing infused with an expensive imported liqueur boasting a fancy foreign name and a sinfully sky-high price tag.

Griff, Von Cartier, and I hop back into the limo and head to the tailor shop to get measured for our tuxedos. Let me tell you, when we arrive, the tailor is quite the character. His hands shake like crazy, which worries me about how our tuxes will turn out. The old man wears thin, silver-toned framed reading glasses hanging from a fancy chain around his wrinkled turkey-like neck, all loose and wobbly. It's like the extra skin has a mind of its own, jiggling about even when he's not talking.

He pushes his glasses up his narrow arched nose as he works —picture Margaret Hamilton in *The Wizard of Oz,* but not so bitchy. He's got this old yellow measuring tape hanging from his neck like it's a fashion statement. It's obvious he's a pro at this measuring stuff. He effortlessly moves the tape and his hands simultaneously while taking measurements. But when measuring the inseam, things start to get weird. His hands seem to be all over the place, except where one would expect them to be. He keeps blabbering about how vital accurate measurements are for a perfect fit. Meanwhile, he's measuring and re-measuring our crotches over and over again. I swear, I've never been so violated and felt up as when that tailor measured me for a pair of pants.

Griff and I don't take the tailor's overly enthusiastic measuring too seriously. The guy is past his prime, and his eyesight could be better. So, we overlook his wandering hands.

After completing the planned tasks for our upcoming ceremony, the limo drops Griff and me off at my condo at the end of the day. As we exit the rented car, Mr. Von Cartier asks Griff a question.

"Mr. Barrows, do you have something to tell me?"

"Whatever do you mean?" a confused Griff asks.

"Have you—you know—told your mother yet?" Mr. Von Cartier persists.

"Not yet," Griff admits. "I haven't had the time."

"Please, for God's sake, keep me informed," Mr. Von Cartier pleads. "I wouldn't want to accidentally blurt out your secret while updating your mother on the progress of the ceremony plans."

Was that a subtle jab at Griff? Or did Von Cartier drop a veiled threat? It's hard to decipher the intentions of a highly-strung, cocktailed queen making a fortune on an event while concealing a significant secret about the grooms from a super-wealthy high-society client.

Why didn't we elope to a place where nobody knew us? We could have had a commitment ceremony practically anywhere. How did our special day turn into this three-ring circus? Oh yeah, Mrs. Rowling-Sakowitz-Goldman-Barrows had to meddle in our business.

Wow! That's my future *mother-in-law*.

CHAPTER 7

Friday evening, August 5
Cornerstone Cathedral Church

Mrs. Jacqueline Rowling-Sakowitz-Goldman-Barrows has gone all out and booked a banquet hall at the Four Seasons for the reception after our ceremony. It's going to be one heck of a party, you know? I can already picture Mr. Von Cartier running around like crazy, ensuring everything is perfect. He's wearing fancy white gloves, carefully examining the crystal stemware for pesky water spots. And let me tell you, he's a pro at arranging the silverware so that every piece lines up perfectly. But man, what a bundle of nerves. I swear, Von Cartier mutters to himself and pops pills from a fancy pill box while buzzing around like a busy bee. I'm exhausted just watching him.

Alright, let's hold our horses. I'm getting ahead of myself. So, before the big reception on Saturday, we must tackle the rehearsal and rehearsal dinner. It's Friday evening, and the ceremony participants gather at Cornerstone Cathedral for the rehearsal. Cal is here, having flown in from California earlier in the day. Joshua and Dexter are also in attendance, along with Griff and his best friend, Stone, who flew in from Dallas. Stone and Griff go way back, having been childhood friends in Dallas. I bet they've got some interesting stories to tell. Unfortunately, there isn't time to get acquainted with Stone because Griff and I are late to arrive. We're running a smidgen late, but Griff insists we're only *fashionably late.*

Mr. Von Cartier, who's in charge, isn't thrilled about our tardiness, especially since it's our own rehearsal. He's clutching a leather notebook stuffed with papers, looking all business-like in his black bespoke suit. He could easily pass for a strict nun in one of those Catholic school movies if he were holding a wooden ruler. The funny thing is, I went to public school, and I'm not Catholic. My idea of Catholic schools and nuns is convoluted because the image in my head comes from what I've seen on TV and in movies.

There's no mistaking that Mr. Von Cartier is in charge, and he doesn't let us forget it. Sometimes, I feel this whole ceremony is more about him than Griff and me. Mrs. Rowling-Sakowitz-Goldman-Barrows had good intentions when she hired him, but he has since gotten on my nerves.

Griff reminds me, *Keep in mind, Mr. Von Cartier has taken on all the chores we'd have had to do ourselves.*

His words bring me some relief. I do appreciate Mrs. Rowling-Sakowitz-Goldman-Barrows for hiring Von Cartier. Had she kept her nose out of our business, none of this would have been necessary. Deep down, I still long for a simple and intimate ceremony, the one that Mrs. Rowling-Sakowitz-Goldman-Barrows stole from Griff and me.

By the way, I haven't had the pleasure of meeting Griff's mom yet. It's like she's this mysterious figure that I can't quite wrap my head around. Griff rarely talks about her, almost as if she's a ghost. But I know she exists because I've seen how Griff's demeanor changes when she speaks to him on the phone. During their conversations, he transforms into a different person, uttering nothing more than a simple *Yes, Mumsy*. His face turns an odd shade of red, and his knuckles turn white. Which is every time Griff talks with her on the phone.

However, I try not to conjure up preconceived notions about her. I don't want to paint her as some ogre in my mind when, in reality, she may be a lovely person. Or at least, that's what I keep telling myself. If I repeat it enough, I might begin to believe it.

So, I have to wait till the ceremony to meet Mrs. Rowling-Sakowitz-Goldman-Barrows. She's a no-show to the rehearsal and the rehearsal dinner. But no worries, Griff assures me she'll definitely attend the ceremony. Griff told me to *look for the largest hat in the sanctuary, and dear ol' Mumsy will be perched under it.*

Regarding the rehearsal, it seems we had no experience with commitment ceremonies. Mr. Von Cartier interrupted the proceedings, meticulously criticizing every detail. His constant interference gave me the worst headache. Griff remained unfazed. Stone, however, made his feelings about Mr. Von Cartier quite clear. His face turned red multiple times, and he clenched his fists. I'm confident he wanted to punch Mr. Von Cartier in the smackeroo on more than one occasion. In fact, there were moments when I thought Stone was going to sock him right there inside the church. Thankfully, Griff managed to pull them apart and prevented a major scene. We witnessed numerous intense stare-downs—like wired alley cats—between Von Cartier and Stone.

Von Cartier has an uncanny ability to effortlessly irritate almost everyone he interacts with. However, Dexter and Joshua found him absolutely hilarious and couldn't help but laugh at the man, snickering at his antics.

After enduring nearly two hours of Von Cartier's mind-numbing instructions, Cal, Stone, Griff, Dexter, Joshua, and I escaped from the church and went to a nearby steakhouse. Initially, the plan was to gather at the Four Seasons for the rehearsal dinner, which Griff's mom generously arranged. However, after being subjected to Von Cartier's never-ending insults and constant put-downs, everyone had had enough of him. So, we quietly slipped from the church without bothering to inform Von Cartier about the change in plans.

Let me tell you, the rest of the evening was a total blast. We couldn't stop laughing, picturing Von Cartier having a hissy fit when he realized we weren't showing up for our own rehearsal dinner at the Four Seasons, which was paid in full and *in advance* by Mrs. Rowling-Sakowitz-Goldman-Barrows. It was the perfect payback shenanigan for putting up with Von

Cartier's long-winded directions and angry, bitchy outbursts.

CHAPTER 8

Saturday morning, August 6
my condo

Today's the big day, and I admit I slept poorly last night. I tossed and turned, thrashing the sheets and covers. It's wild how Griff can sleep soundly through anything. Once his head hits the pillow, he's out until morning. Meanwhile, I wasn't able to sleep. I'm a bundle of raw nerves, unable to sit at the breakfast nook to enjoy my coffee.

At the moment, it's just Griff and me at the condo. He crashed here last night. The boys are sleeping at their apartment like they usually do on weekends. They need their beauty sleep after last night's rehearsal dinner/bachelor party. This morning feels weird without them devouring breakfast faster than I can serve it. Griff and I had a quiet breakfast—just the two of us. The dirty dishes sit on the table as we leisurely sip our coffee. The condo is too calm for my taste. I miss the laughter and playful banter the boys bring to the table.

I remember that this isn't any ordinary Saturday morning. It's the day of my commitment ceremony to my partner—Griff. With a coffee mug in hand, I glance across the bartop at the newspaper Griff is hiding behind.

"Don't you think it's time we start getting ready?" I ask.

Silence comes from the other side of the newspaper.

"Griff?" I repeat.

A faint grunt emerges from behind the morning paper.

"Perhaps I should phone the boys to make sure they don't oversleep," I say.

I wait for a response from Griff which doesn't come. I might as well be talking to myself.

Speaking of the phone, it suddenly rings. Griff jumps up and grabs it, displaying lightning-fast reflexes. I remember him mentioning that he was redirecting his calls to my place in case something should come up. What would we do without technology, you know?

"Hello," he chirps into the receiver, then nods several times; with each nod, his face grows redder and redder. After a few moments, his expression transforms into one of fury.

"Fine," he snaps before forcefully slamming the phone onto its cradle.

"Was that your mom?" I inquire, knowing precisely who the caller was because she's the only person I know who can get under his skin that way.

"Yup," Griff responds, snatching the newspaper and angrily flipping through the pages.

"Is she on her way?" I continue, trying to make conversation.

"Yup," he replies, not giving additional information.

"Is she flying in?" I inquire, eager to gather more details.

"Yup," he grunts, his attention still divided, not fully invested in our conversation.

"Just so you know, I'm eloping with Cal. Is that cool with you?" I throw it out there, waiting to see how he reacts.

"Yup," he replies, void of any emotion or surprise.

The room sinks into an oppressive silence that makes me feel as if I'm all alone.

After approximately three prolonged beats, the newspaper crinkles.

Griff's curious eyes rise over the top of the paper to stare oddly at me.

"What did you say?" he asks.

"Finally," I say with a hint of satisfaction, "I've got your attention."

"I'm sorry, I wasn't listening," Griff's expression softens.

"Ya think?" I tease.

"What were you saying?" He looks genuinely puzzled.

I lean in closer, wanting to satisfy my nosiness.

"Was that your mom on the phone?" I ask.

"Yeah," Griff says. "She called to tell me—us—that she's waiting for her plane at Dallas Love Field airport."

Griff buries his head back into the newspaper.

"Is she really taking a commercial flight?" I ask.

"No way, Jose!" Griff exclaims from behind his newspaper. "Mrs. Rowling-Sakowitz-Goldman-Barrows fly commercial? That's never going to happen, not in a million years. She's in the terminal, waiting for her private plane."

"Must be nice to be rich," I say, then gulp down the last of my coffee.

"Was there anything else?" I inquire. "You know, like, did she ask about me?"

Griff peeks from behind the newspaper.

"She's looking forward to meeting you," Griff says.

"Did she say that, or are you trying to make me believe she cares a flip about me?"

"Okay, I said that to shut you up."

"Finally, something I can believe," I chuckle.

The mere thought of meeting Mrs. Rowling-Sakowitz-Goldman-Barrows ties my stomach in knots. And to add to the stress, Griff still hasn't come out to his mom. I have this sinking feeling that by him keeping his homosexuality a secret from his mom, things won't end well. After the ceremony, I can imagine how Mrs. Rowling-Sakowitz-Goldman-Barrows might react to her son having a *husband* instead of a wife.

And what about grandkids? All new mother-in-laws want grandkids. Right? We've got that covered. I'm bringing two boys into the relationship, so we'll be an instant family of four. Mrs. Rowling-Sakowitz-Goldman-Barrows will have instant grandkids—grown boys, but still grandkids. I hope she's open to having grandkids because whether she likes it or not, she's getting them. Dexter, Joshua, and I are a package deal, and that's how it is. Good lord, I'm already making demands on my mother-in-law-to-be, and I haven't even met her.

I have no idea why I'm thinking about this stuff. It's probably nerves, you know. But I can't help but feel she's a stuck-up, snobby busybody. I know that's no way to talk about my soon-to-be mother-in-law. She'll be my mother-in-law in a few hours, whether I like it or not, and visa-versa. I only hope she doesn't turn out to be a witch with a broomstick stuck up her... well, you know.

"Griff, what's the newspaper say about today's weather forecast?" I ask.

"It says *sunny and hot* like it's been for weeks," Griff replies. "Why do you ask?"

"Oh, just wondering," I chuckle. "I had this crazy image in my head of a house getting sucked up into a tornado and then spit out on Mrs. Rowling-Sakowitz-Goldman-Barrows. Only her fancy stockings and ruby slippers stick out from under the house."

Griff smirks and shakes his head.

After putting the breakfast dishes in the dishwasher, I call Cal at his hotel room. Let's face it: who can trust those hotel wake-up calls? So, I dial his number and patiently wait for an answer. And I wait. And wait. And wait a little longer. Finally, after an eternity, Cal answers the phone, sounding completely out of breath.

"Yo," he blurts between gasps of air.

"Morning, Cal," I say. "You sound like you just ran a marathon. Are you returning from your morning run?"

"You could say I had a workout of sorts," Cal replies, struggling to catch his breath.

That's a strange response. I think to myself, but hey, who am I to judge?

"I'm your morning wake-up call," I explain. "You were the life of the party last night, so I wanted to make sure you're alive and well this morning."

"I'm fine," Cal reassures me. "Seriously, I'm better than fine, I'm fantastic."

Phew, that's a relief. At least he's not nursing a hangover.

"Well, Griff and I are about to get ready," I say.

"We'll be doing the same," Cal responds.

"We? As in more than just yourself?" I ask.

"Oops, did I say too much?" Cal snickers.

"Is there someone else with you?" I inquire.

"No," Cal adamantly denies. "Why would you think that?"

"Come on, Cal," I say. "I'm pretty sure I heard another voice besides yours."

"Okay," Cal admits. "I guess you'll find out eventually."

"Find out what?" I ask, genuinely curious.

"Stone and I kind of hooked up last night."

"Stone?" I ask. "As in Griff's best friend, Stone?"

Mind you, I'm not pissed, just surprised.

"Kind of—" Cal says.

"Do you plan on telling Griff?" I ask.

"I believe that's Stone's responsibility to break that kind of news with his best friend," Cal says.

I've no idea how Griff will react to such a revelation. Moreover, Stone is an adult capable of making his own decisions. However, what about his girlfriend back in Dallas? I assumed Stone was straight since he spoke—several times—of his girlfriend last night. Maybe he's bisexual, which is a possibility. Then again, Stone may be exploring his options before settling into married life. Alternatively, it's conceivable that Stone was so intoxicated last night that Cal took advantage of him. Oh my, what if Griff blames Cal for *turning* his best friend gay? That is utterly absurd. However, on a day like today, my gay commitment ceremony, I suppose anything's possible.

"Hey, Shane?" Cal's voice comes through the phone. "Are you still there?"

"Yeah, I'm here."

"Sorry, buddy. I didn't mean to dump on your special day."

"We'll catch up later, alright?" I say.

"Sure thing," he says, then hangs up.

Thanks a bunch, Cal, I mutter to myself. It's just another worry to add to the list on the most important day of my life.

CHAPTER 9

Saturday afternoon, August 6
Cornerstone Cathedral Church

When Griff and I arrive at the church, Von Cartier charges toward the limo like a freshly branded raging bull. Grabbing hold of the door handle, he swings open the door.

"Where the heck have you two been?" he screams at us, his face red with frustration. "Do you have any idea how late you are?"

Griff, always cool as a cucumber (unless talking to his mom), calmly responds as he steps out of the stretch limo parked by the side entrance to the church.

"We're not *that* late," he tells Von Cartier, offering his hand to me and assisting me out of the vehicle.

Yesterday, during the rehearsal, Von Cartier made it crystal clear that the ceremony party WILL discreetly enter the church through the side door. This way, the guests won't see us before the ceremony. Let me tell you, Von Cartier is so theatrical about everything. Trust me when I say Von Cartier is the queen of drama queens. He makes a huge fuss about every little thing. I suppose that's why he rakes in the big bucks.

Surprisingly, he doesn't mention how we ditched him after last night's ceremony rehearsal. He's probably already grilled the other members of the ceremony party while waiting for Griff and me.

"Are Cal and Stone here?" I inquire as Griff, Von Cartier, and I enter the church from the side door.

"No, they're not," Von Cartier replies, glancing at his flashy gold wristwatch adorned with sparkling diamonds. "We're the only ones here."

I exchange an anxious glance with Griff.

181

"Don't worry," Griff gives my hand a reassuring pat. "Queens are notorious for our fashionably late entrances."

That makes me wonder about Stone, though. The thought of him and Cal together baffles me. I thought, for sure, Stone was straight, or at least until this morning when Cal accidentally revealed otherwise.

"It's true, Stone was never on time as a kid," Griff chuckles. "Stone might just as well be gay."

Joking or not, maybe Griff knows more about Stone than he's letting on. I think to myself. *Could there be a romantic history between Stone and Griff? I scold myself for trying to blow things out of proportion. Don't I have enough to worry about without conjuring up a potential past romance between Griff and Stone? Besides, I'm the one who will be walking down the aisle with Griff, not Stone. Yet, Stone is Griff's best man, so he will accompany Griff. But, I'm leaving today's ceremony with a ring on my finger—Stone will not.*

Good Lord, I really need a Xanax right about now.

Von Cartier nervously paces back and forth like a caged mountain lion, muttering to himself. Frequently checking his watch will not make time miraculously stop until the entire party is present and accounted for. He's seriously driving me crazy.

The side door bursts open.

Von Cartier lets out a sigh of relief.

Instead of Stone and Cal, Dexter and Joshua rush in like determined firefighters on their way to put out a fire.

"Someone forgot to set the alarm," Dexter accuses, shooting Joshua a dirty expression.

"Hey, sorry we're late," Joshua announces, wrinkling his nose at an annoyed Von Cartier.

"You see," I elbow Griff in the ribs and whisper to him, "I should have called them, but no..."

"It's not a big deal. We thought you were Stone and Cal," Griff remarks.

"Sorry to disappoint you," Dexter scowls, placing his hands on his hips.

"Dex," Griff interjects, "that's not a flattering look for you."

Looking at himself, Dexter blushes, then adjusts his posture to a more masculine stance.

"So, where are Cal and Stone?" Joshua asks.

"That's the million-dollar question," I say as I manage a worried smile. "Unfortunately, we're completely clueless."

"Man, I was freaking out, thinking we'd be late," Joshua says. "And we beat the best men here."

A tense silence thickens.

I take a good, long look at Joshua and Dexter.

Damn, they look all grown up in their tuxes. I think to myself. *It's like I haven't seen them in ages, or maybe I just haven't seen them for who they are. In my mind, I see them as happy-go-lucky high school boys.*

"Look at you guys, all spiffed up," I say, grinning at Joshua and Dexter. "You've turned out to be quite the young men."

"Aw, come on," Joshua blushes.

"Don't stop on my account," Dexter says, smirking and strutting like he's the cock of the walk.

"I'll smack you if you don't stop that," Joshua threatens.

"Alright, boys, that's enough," I step in, playing the role of a responsible step-uncle. A step-uncle they ignore, considering they're in their early twenties.

How did time fly so quickly? I think to myself. *It seems like yesterday when these boys were high school sophomores kicking around a soccer ball. Look at them now—grown men, or at least almost. I honestly couldn't be prouder of them.*

"Yoo-hoo! Anyone home?" a gravelly, falsetto voice echoes from the hall.

I assume the voice belongs to Mumsy Barrows, Griff's mom.

"We're in here!" Von Cartier calls out, pushing his way to greet the latecomer.

Nervous, I quickly pat my hair to ensure it's in place and adjust my bow tie. I must make a killer first impression on my future mother-in-law. I rub the tops of my shoes against the back of my pant legs, ensuring no dust. This moment has to be flawless, like a perfectly cut diamond. I stand tall and straight, just like I used to do as a kid when Momma measured my height against the kitchen door frame. Each tick mark represented a new milestone in my journey of growing taller, like stepping stones on the path of life.

The room goes dead silent as the excitement and tension build. Suddenly, this massive woman struts into the room. She's definitely not what I expected, that's for certain. Yet, there's something about her that feels strangely familiar.

Then, she winks at me, and a wrinkle creases the corner of her bright red-painted lips.

I can't believe my eyes—the person before me is not Mrs. Rowling-Sakowitz-Goldman-Barrows. I can't control myself; I burst into hysterical laughter. I'm shocked and stumble over my words, trying to understand what's happening. "What? How?" I manage to blurt out. "What the heck are you doing here?"

"Shane. Shane. Shane," the new arrival says, "you're still as high-strung as always. Why don't you sit and relax while I spill the tea."

"Dad?" Joshua blurts. "Is that you?"

"Yes, son, it's me," the unnamed visitor responds, spreading hairy arms wide and inviting Joshua into a huge hug.

"I can't believe it's really you, and you're actually here," Joshua exclaims, returning the hug with equal excitement.

Dexter stands quietly on the sideline, taking everything in. A shit-eating grin splits his face as he shakes his head.

"I can't believe you're here," I interject, taking small sips of water from a paper cup Griff mysteriously conjured out of thin air like a skilled magician.

"Shane, you didn't think I'd miss your big day, did you?" the visitor remarks, followed by a tight bear hug.

"But how did you know?" I ask, eager for an answer.

"Josh keeps me updated through his letters," the visitor explains.

I finish the water, wad the cup, and pitch it in the trash, all the time intrigued by the unexpected visitor's presence.

"Dad, why are you wearing a dress?" Joshua asks, unable to contain his curiosity.

"Well, that's what I'm about to explain," the visitor replies with a mischievous twinkle in his eyes.

Suddenly, the outside door bursts open, and Cal rushes in.

"I'm here," Cal announces, gasping for breath. "The ceremony can begin."

Cal slams on the brakes, and his mouth hangs open in shock. He can't tear his eyes away from the sight before him—a large man wearing an insane amount of Estée Lauder makeup and a chiffon cocktail dress that not even the most fearless drag queen would wear.

"What the hell? Who's this?" Cal blurts out, eyes bulging and voice echoing. He searches the faces in the room for someone—anyone who can answer his question.

I step up, fully intending to smooth things over.

"Uh, Cal, I'd like you to meet my ex-boyfriend, Kip."

Griff elbows me in the ribs while hiding a mischievous grin spreading across his face. Leaning in, he whispers to me.

"Is this the same ex-boyfriend who's supposed to be in prison?" Griff asks.

"Indeed, one and the same," Kip responds with a broad, toothy smile, inadvertently revealing a smear of red lipstick on his front teeth.

Von Cartier, visibly overwhelmed, sinks into a chair and hastily retrieves a fancy hand fan from his tuxedo pocket. Fanning vigorously, he desperately seeks relief from the sudden surprises.

"I believe I require a thorough explanation," Von Cartier says, his voice tinged with bewilderment and exasperation.

"Alright," Kip says, "let me start from the beginning—"

"If you don't mind, can we please have the Cliff Notes?" Cal pleads. "We've got a commitment ceremony to get on with."

"Here's the deal," Kip explains. "When I found out Shane

was tying the knot in a commitment ceremony, I knew I had to be here."

"But," Dexter interjects, "aren't you supposed to be in the State Pen?"

"Yeah." Kip nods. "But I obviously can't be in two places at once, now, can I?"

"So, Dad," Joshua asks, "how did you get here?"

"I took a taxi, of course," Kip grins.

"A three hundred mile taxi ride?" Joshua asks.

"Forget the taxi," Cal interrupts. "Did you escape from the pen?"

"Of course, I broke out," Kip says smugly.

"But how?" I ask.

"That's a story for another time," Kip replies. "For now, let's assume I'm a fugitive on the run."

"Ah," Dexter interjects, "that's why you're dressed in drag. It's your disguise."

"You catch on fast, Dex," Kip remarks.

"Dad, aren't you taking a huge risk by being here?" Joshua asks.

"Yes, son," Kip opens up, "but it's worth it. When Shane and I were together, I didn't give him what he deserved—a commitment ceremony. Today, I'm here to make up for that and share in this momentous occasion."

"That's incredibly sweet," I add, touched by Kip's gesture.

However, Kip isn't finished. He turns to me and declares, "But that's not all. I'm also here to be YOUR best man."

"Best man?" Cal scoffs. "Please tell me, you're joking, right? Best men don't wear a 50s cocktail frock, a mussed up Doris Day wig, high-heel pumps, and enough eye shadow to make a rock star jealous."

"I'm dead serious, I fully intend to be Shane's best man," Kip responds firmly. "Wearing a tux is absolutely not an option for me. I'd be instantly recognized and hauled away in handcuffs before the ceremony even starts."

"Sounds good to me," Cal snickers.

"Hold everything," Von Cartier interrupts, wiping sweat off his forehead, "are you suggesting that there are police officers among the guests?"

"Heavens, no—not cops," Kip shakes his head.

"Thank goodness for small blessings," Von Cartier sighs in relief.

"I believe they prefer to be called State Police," Cal corrects.

"Oh my, Mother Mary of God, have mercy,' Von Cartier exclaims while crossing himself. After which, he melts into a chair.

"How I see it, once the State Police catches wind of my true identity in this disguise, the ceremony will have already been over," Kip remarks. "If I'm lucky, they won't recognize me until after the reception. All I truly want is to walk down the aisle with Shane as his best man," Kip adds earnestly, studying my expression.

"No frickin' chance, buddy," Cal bellows. "I'm Shane's best man. He specifically asked me. I didn't barge in and force myself into the ceremony. Unlike some tacky-ass drag queens, we know." Cal gets his point across by pounding an index finger into Kip's breastbone.

Jeez, the atmosphere is saturated with testosterone. I never thought I'd see the day Cal would fight over me, especially with my ex-boyfriend. I assumed Griff would be jealous in this situation, but nope, he might as well be watching from the sidelines with a bag of popcorn and a large coke. All the while, my best friend Cal is being possessive as hell and has no intention of sharing me with Kip.

I take a deep breath and pause to gather my thoughts.

"Hey, Cal," I say, trying to reason with him. "Kip's situation is complicated. He risked getting caught to come here. Look, he's made it this far. Hasn't he earned his place in the ceremony?"

Cal shoots me his signature *what-the-hell?-look*, an expression I'd seen countless times in high school.

"Mr. Von Cartier, is there a rule that says I can't have both a *best man* and a *best ex-boyfriend*?" I ask.

"I suppose not," Von Cartier stutters, shaking his head in resignation. "It's your ceremony, after all. Do whatever you want."

I catch Cal muttering something under his breath.

"Cal, do you have something to say?" I ask.

Shaking his head, Cal leaves me wondering what he's up to.

"Griff has a fifty percent say in this ceremony," I say. "If Griff is okay with Kip being my *best ex-boyfriend*, I'm cool. What do you say, Griff?"

"Whatever you want," Griff shrugs, "I'm good with whatever you want."

Earlier, when Cal first arrived at the church, had he gotten his way, Kip would have been buried six feet under the church before the ceremony started. I have absolutely no idea what got into Cal. Usually, he's easygoing and agreeable.

Then, onto another pressing matter, we still need a best man for Griff—Stone is still MIA.

CHAPTER 10

Saturday afternoon, August 6
Cornerstone Cathedral Church

Let me tell you, Mumsy Barrows couldn't have chosen a more sweltering day for our commitment ceremony. The air is so sticky with humidity that one can practically wring it from clothes. The sun is scorching down on us like we're stranded in the Sahara desert. Don't get me wrong, the sky is a stunning shade of blue, with those fluffy white clouds leisurely drifting by. But I long for an occasional refreshing, cool breeze. If today's temperature doesn't go in the history books as the hottest day on record, I swear it'll tie as the second hottest.

Before Mumsy Barrows entered the picture, my initial plan for our commitment ceremony was to avoid the afternoon heat by having a morning event. I mean, let's be real: who wants to be drenched in sweat while witnessing two gay guys exchange vows? So, naturally, I chose a morning affair. But no, Mrs. Rowling-Sakowitz-Goldman-Barrows insisted on a mid-afternoon ceremony, leaving everyone to melt in the Texas humidity and heat.

Furthermore, Mrs. Rowling-Sakowitz-Goldman-Barrows assured us that the church is equipped with air conditioning, so there's no need to be concerned about the outside temperature.

What does she know about Austin weather? By lunchtime, the temperature outside soared to a scorching 100 degrees, if not hotter. Come on, this is summer in Texas. It's a little after 2 pm, and who knows how high the temperature will climb before suppertime. As guests walk from the parking lot to the church, they become drenched in sweat. How inconvenient is that?

Griff shared a little secret about Mrs. Rowling-Sakowitz-Goldman-Barrows, which shed light on why she chose an

189

afternoon event. Apparently, dear ol' Mumsy requires *at least ten hours of beauty sleep,* which explains why she never schedules anything before noon.

Just between you and me, she reminds me of some pampered drag queens I know.

Let's rewind the clock a few minutes to when Griff, Joshua, Dexter, Cal, Kip, Von Cartier, and I waited for Stone to show up. As I mentioned before, Stone was a no-show. The clock was ticking, and it was way past time to start the ceremony. Sadly, Griff had no best man. On the other hand, I was lucky enough to have both a best man and a best ex-boyfriend.

"Hey, Cal," I suggest, "why don't you step in as Griff's best man? Kip, you can be my best man."

"No offense to Griff," Cal says while shaking his head, "I flew in from California to be your best man, and that's exactly what I intend to be."

"Come on, Cal," I plead, feeling the pressure to get this show on the road. "We've got to start the ceremony. Griff needs a best man so that we can start."

"I've already told you. I'm not doing it," Cal says firmly.

"Please," I beg, desperation creeping into my voice.

Cal is momentarily quiet; I hope he's weighing his options.

"Alright, fine," Cal concedes. "I'll do this as a favor to you, Shane."

"Thanks a lot," I say, genuinely grateful for Cal's sacrifice.

Cal and Griff assume their positions to begin the walk down the aisle. Kip and I are behind them, patiently waiting our turn to follow suit. Dexter and Joshua are behind Kip and me. The boys don't have designated duties in the ceremony. Griff and I added them to the procession because they begged to participate in the ceremony.

Kip meticulously adjusts his wig, using a mirrored compact, ensuring it is centered.

Meanwhile, I straighten my bow tie.

Suddenly, the church's side door, facing the street, swings open. Stone storms inside, his face red, and his breath comes in heavy gasps.

"Sorry, I'm late," Stone pants, trying to catch his breath. "My bad, man. Today hasn't been my day. I got locked out of my room, lost my key, and phoned the church, but there was no answer, then I couldn't get a damn cab. I ended up sprinting from the hotel."

"How did you lose your key?" Griff asks. "Where did you go?"

"It's late," I quickly say to Griff, hoping to derail this conversation. "Let's not get into that right now, okay?"

"But?" Griff asks, cocking his head.

"Stone, you made it just in time," I say, pushing Stone into place beside Griff.

"Hey man, who's the tired drag queen?" Stone whispers to Kip while wiping sweat from his neck with a handkerchief.

"Oh, that's Shane's ex," Cal whispers. "It's a long story. I'll fill you in later."

Cal scowls at Kip, nudging him with a not-so-gentle shove, almost toppling him off his towering high-heel pumps.

Kip stumbles out of line, leaving an empty slot next to me.

Not wasting time, Cal glides into the newly vacated place.

"No way, you're not bullying me out of my rightful place next to Shane," Kip snaps at Cal, forcefully pushing Cal aside while swinging his pocketbook like a kettlebell.

"I'm Shane's best man," Cal says to Kip, grabbing the threatening pocketbook.

"Quit acting all high and mighty," Cal says, shoving Kip aside and claiming the newly vacated spot beside me.

"For Christ's sake, will the two of you stop acting like spoiled brats and grow up?" Von Cartier interrupts, patting beads of sweat from his forehead with a fistful of tissues. "Hey, you," Von Cartier points to Kip, "you in the dress—stand on Shane's right, and Cal, you stand on Shane's left."

"Well, well, looks like I'm Shane's best man after all," Kip smirks at Cal, linking his arm with mine.

Cal pulls Kip and me apart, then wraps my arm with his.

"Seriously, don't even try me, you jailbird floozy," Cal says to Kip.

Kip puffs up, and his face turns crimson.

"What the hell did you call me, you washed-up high school jock?" Kip fires back at Cal.

"You heard me—you tired ol' drag queen," Cal spits. "If the shoe fits—or in your case, the pumps—they're big enough to fit Mother Hubbard and her whole damn brood."

Kip winds his pocketbook by the handle, aiming for Cal.

"Boys! Girls!" Von Cartier says, positioning himself between Cal and Kip's pocketbook. "Do I need to remind you we're in a church? Can we keep things civil? Please?"

Someone should tell Von Cartier that it's not a good idea for one to come between two gay guys about to get into a bitch-slapping brawl.

"Hey, guys, I've got an idea," Von Cartier suggests. "How about both of you be *best men* for Shane? We can settle this without violence—as civilized men." Von Cartier throws a challenging glare at Cal, then at Kip.

No one moves in the silence as Von Cartier stares down the two foes.

Kip extends a hand of momentary neutrality to Cal.

Cal studies Kip's hand before accepting Kip's handshake offer.

The shake doesn't represent world peace but brings a brief reprieve from the fighting.

After which, both men put distance between each other.

Exhausted, Von Cartier plops into a chair and starts fanning himself with a hand fan.

I suppose it took an incredible amount of energy for Von Cartier to act butch to defuse the tense situation between Kip and Cal. It must have exhausted him physically and emotionally, leaving him utterly drained.

Von Cartier takes advantage of the momentary reprieve to

pop a pill, gulping it down without water. He takes a few deep breaths before suddenly springing from his chair in a burst of newfound energy.

"It's showtime!" Von Cartier sings while clapping his hands for emphasis. Making a big sweeping gesture, he directs us to put on huge smiles while pointing to his own forced grin that's anything but genuine. He then nods to the organist.

The elderly woman stops playing some boring hymn on the pipe organ, replacing it with a loud, resounding chord. This grandiose note reverberates through the very foundation of the church, serving as a signal for the commencement of the ceremony. The congregation grows silent and alert.

Let me tell you, when it comes to gays hosting a fabulous gay social gathering, being punctual is not exactly our strong suit. But despite the unexpected drama before our event, we're managing quite well. Surprisingly, our ceremony is running about thirty minutes behind schedule—okay, so it's probably closer to forty-five or fifty minutes late, which is par for the course.

Stone and Griff strut down the center aisle, setting the pace as the commitment party makes our way to the front of the sanctuary. Cal, Kip, and I follow, taking our turn down the aisle. As we proceed, I notice the State Police officers strategically positioned at each exit, and how they don't blend well into the surroundings.

I turn to Kip.

He's sporting a wide grin from ear to ear. Long, dazzling cut glass earrings bounce and shimmer with every step Kip takes in his oversized pumps. I chuckle at his swollen feet, resembling rising bread dough that has risen beyond the confines of their baking pans.

Taking a quick scan of the sanctuary, I notice that every pew is jam-packed. To my right are the fancy rich folks, Mrs. Rowling-Sakowitz-Goldman-Barrows' esteemed guests, looking all posh and important. It's a different story to my left, with Griff and my friends filling those seats. Let me tell you, everyone is dressed to impress. The ladies are rocking stylish summer outfits with over-the-top hats covered in flowers, ribbons, and scarves. And the men decked out in snazzy suits, complete with boutonnieres. But here's the kicker: I notice a striking difference between the guests on the right and those on the left when I look closer.

What's the difference, you ask?

The lady guests on the left are actually men dressed in women's clothing. It's difficult to determine who's wearing more makeup–the drag queens or their gay male escorts. Suddenly, a wave of panic comes over me. I'm reminded of the nightclub scene from the 1978 film *La Cage aux Folles*, brimming with flamboyant and extravagant personalities. I scan the sanctuary, desperately searching for *Zaza Napoli*.

Kip senses my impending panic attack and gently squeezes my hand, offering reassurance.

I smile back.

Throughout our time together as boyfriends, he had a knack for calming me down, even before I realized the signs of an approaching anxiety attack. Kip and I made a fantastic couple, and we would still be together if it weren't for the unfortunate circumstances surrounding his arrest due to trumped-up fake charges.

As Kip releases his grip on my hand, I sense I'm starting to calm down. All this time, Cal, Kip, and I have been making our way toward the front of the church. Passing by the front pew, I crane my neck, attempting to get a look at my future mother-in-law. Unfortunately, her ginormous floppy summer hat blocks my view of her face.

So, there we are, Cal, Kip, and I, joining Stone and Griff, Dexter and Joshua, bringing up the rear, and all of us are at the front of the church. Cal gives me a firm handshake while Kip wraps me in a bear hug so tight I'm concerned about bruised ribs. Stone exchanges a friendly handshake with Griff. The three best men and the boys step out of the spotlight. Now, it's just

Griff, the officiant, and me standing in front of a sanctuary packed with folks invited to celebrate our incredible gay commitment ceremony.

"Welcome, everyone," the officiating person announces warmly, a smile lighting up his face. "Today, we come together to witness the joyous union of Shane and Griffen as they declare their undying love for one another."

Suddenly, a loud gasp echoes through the sanctuary. Curious, I turn toward the congregation to see what the commotion is all about. To my surprise, Mrs. Rowling-Sakowitz-Goldman-Barrows slumps to her side; thankfully, she's seated, so there's no danger of physical harm.

Von Cartier rushes to her side, fanning her and calling for a doctor.

In true drag fashion, the drag queens join in, adding exaggerated screeches and pretend gasps to the spectacle. It's quite a scene, with lace hankies dabbing at imaginary tears. Keep in mind that real tears would ruin the drag queen's flawless makeup.

The lesson here: A drag queen will never allow a straight heterosexual woman to upstage them at any time.

I need a moment to collect my thoughts, so I close my eyes and silently hope for a miracle. And when I open my eyes, guess what I see? A bunch of frantic high society snobs huddled around Mrs. Rowling-Sakowitz-Goldman-Barrows crowded in the vicinity of the front pew. Amid the chaos, a doctor is doing his best to revive Mrs. Rowling-Sakowitz-Goldman-Barrows with smelling salts and slapping her cheeks—the cheeks on her face—get your mind out of the gutter.

"Aren't you going to go over there to be with your mother?" I say to Griff.

"Why?" Griff says. "She's being taken care of."

"You didn't tell her, did you?" I ask Griff in a hushed tone.

"Well," he whispers back, "I didn't get around to it."

And that's how Griff came out to his mother—during our fabulous gay commitment ceremony. The moment Mrs. Rowling-Sakowitz-Goldman-Barrows noticed no bride standing beside her son at the altar, she suddenly realized that her son might be—you know—a homosexual. I must admit, the lady deserves some credit—she was remarkably perceptive.

After Mrs. Rowling-Sakowitz-Goldman-Barrows regained consciousness and collected herself, the ceremony proceeded. The mother of the first groom—Griff—was seated in the front pew and expressed her emotions in wailing sobs.

Von Cartier sat next to her, attempting to console her.

She swatted at him each time he touched her as if he were an annoying housefly.

The ceremony ends with the officiant introducing groom one (Griff) and groom two (me) to the congregation as Mr. Griffin Darnell Barrows and Mr. Shane Aaron Davison. As the words linger in the air, the organist strikes a powerful chord that echoes throughout the entire church, making the building tremble and, no doubt, waking the dead. The congregation (Griff and my friends) erupt in cheers and applause. The only thing missing was a sparkling fireworks show.

Griff and I are poised to walk down the aisle to exit the church as a fully committed same-sex couple. We have this fantastic vision of leaving the church while dozens and dozens of white doves gracefully fly above us. It's to be a truly magical moment. However, in reality, things take an unexpected turn.

Picture Griff and me as we're about to walk down the aisle; a loud bang, resembling a gunshot, comes from the balcony. I look up, and to my surprise, a cloud of white doves go absolutely bat-shit crazy above our heads inside the church. The birds frantically flap their wings, darting about in the sanctuary as if possessed. Feathers fly thick in the air like a whiteout winter blizzard. Not to mention the poop bombs the doves are strategically releasing from above the guest's heads.

Our invited guests screech, scream, and scramble for safety to escape the deranged birds. The feathered assailants swoop down upon the crowd. In contrast, others collide with the exquisite stained-glass windows, unleashing chaos within our guests. It's akin to a spine-chilling horror flick come to life. I'm telling you, it's pandemonium with a capital P. Mr. Hitchcock would have loved the mayhem.

The congregation screams and yells as the crazed birds attack from above. Our meticulously planned magical moment dive bombs into a complete nightmare.

Those out-of-control birds were supposed to have been released into the outdoors from a balcony window. They were—in theory—supposed to have flown over Griff and my heads as we stepped outside the church. Initially, the experience was to have been fairytale-like, just like in an enchanting Disney movie. However, those feathered demons had different ideas, as if they had a personal grudge against our commitment ceremony.

Meanwhile, Mrs. Rowling-Sakowitz-Goldman-Barrows desperately whacks at the relentless attacking birds as her elegant, high-class guests panic and scramble for safety. As for Von Cartier, he's passed out cold on the floor, speckled in dove droppings. Don't even try to picture that. It's an image you won't get out of your mind anytime soon. Trust me.

The drag queens recreate select scenes from Alfred Hitchcock's *The Birds*. It's like a talent show at the gay clubs, where each drag queen is trying to outshine others as if there's a fabulous prize up for grabs.

Those poor birds must have been absolutely terrified. Instead of gracefully gliding through the open skies, they caused chaos inside the church. And who can we blame for this bird cataclysmic calamity? I'm pointing my finger at my new mother-in-law, Mrs. Rowling-Sakowitz-Goldman-Barrows. After all, she was the one who insisted on having *innocent white doves, dozens and dozens*, she said.

Now, mind you, I can't solely blame Mrs. Rowling-

Sakowitz-Goldman-Barrows for this whole debacle because, let's be honest, if it weren't for those dang birds, none of this craziness would have happened. Seriously, who would've thought a loud chord played on a pipe organ would scare them out of their feathers? I suppose we could sue; after all, those birds were *hired professionals*, paid to exit through a balcony window into the great outdoors and soar over Griff and me as we left the church. Instead, they went rogue, causing chaos and wreaking the conclusion of our commitment ceremony. Clearly, that was a breach of contract. Am I right? Or am I right?

Let's not dwell on what could've or should've been. We can't change what's done. The misfortune certainly added a distinctive twist to our special day. Who, other than Griff and I, can say they had a Hitchcockian moment at their gay commitment ceremony? I'm sure it's one of those stories that will be told repeatedly for years. If not, it should be. Am I right?

Despite how things unfolded at our ceremony's conclusion, there's a lesson to be learned. Whether it's a heterosexual wedding or a gay commitment ceremony, being prepared for the unexpected is crucial. May I recommend distributing disposable rain caps *beforehand* if you intend to invite live birds to your event?

CHAPTER 11

Saturday late afternoon, August 6
Four Seasons

Our commitment ceremony was just the first of unfortunate events on our special day, like a chain reaction of falling dominoes. Once the first domino fell, everything else followed suit, resulting in a complete disaster of a day. It's not unusual to face a few obstacles when hosting an event. Still, it seemed like our ceremony day was cursed with more setbacks than torn holes in an old knitted sweater after a heated catfight.

After the disastrous gay commitment ceremony, our reception is Von Cartier's big chance to redeem himself and showcase his skills as the top-notch Wedding Planner to the Stars. Unfortunately, things are about to sour.

Entering the Four Seasons reception hall, we're greeted by the aftermath of a little girl's birthday party. The venue is filled with an overabundance of pink:

- Pink crepe paper streamers
- Pink balloons
- Pink party plates
- Pink drinking cups
- Even pink tablecloths on tiny children's pink tables and chairs

It's as if Barbie herself had exploded in the reception hall. Von Cartier is not pleased with the condition of the venue. The reception hall differs from what he had arranged with the hotel booking agent. This sends him into hyper-drive and running a muck while gobbling pills like they're candy mints. It's pretty evident he's losing grasp of reality.

Poor, exasperated Mrs. Rowling-Sakowitz-Goldman-Barrows squeezes herself into one of those itty-bitty children's chairs, bawling her eyes out. Her fancy high-society friends huddle in the shadows, scared and bewildered.

The society reporters from several of the surrounding states most prominent newspapers have a field day at Mrs. Rowling-Sakowitz-Goldman-Barrow's expense, reporting on the tanking of what was touted as the pinnacle of high society's social season for the wealthy Texas elite.

Our ceremony day is turning into a total disaster. Von Cartier had a golden opportunity to redeem himself with the reception. Still, fate was dead set on making him appear incompetent and humiliating Griff and me even more.

Amidst the chaos, Von Cartier barks orders at the staff, demanding they fix the reception hall. Surprisingly, the gay guests rush in, eager to lend a helping hand to salvage the reception hall in any way they can.

Lucky for us, one of our guests is a professional disc jockey at a popular local gay disco. He hauls an impressive assortment of records and turntables from the trunk of his car into the reception hall. In no time, he starts spinning captivating tunes that ignite energy among the gay guests. It's almost as if the DJ's music taps into a hidden well of vitality, transforming the reception hall into a lively scene reminiscent of a bustling Saturday night at a gay disco.

Once the children's tables and chairs are swapped out for suitable adult-sized furniture, the guests take their seats for the reception dinner. The waitstaff, dressed in fine attire, gracefully navigate the hall, serving reception dinner dishes to the delight of the guests. The staff's movements are so precise and coordinated that it feels like watching a ballet performance. Von Cartier oversees the waitstaff, ensuring every dinner plate is delivered with utmost care and precision.

The reception is back on track. Von Cartier is pleased, and Mrs. Rowling-Sakowitz-Goldman-Barrows smiles and visits cheerfully with her snooty friends.

A waiter briskly passes by me with a dinner plate in each raised hand. I do a double-take when I see what's on the plates. French fries, a hot dog, and a side of pork and beans? Seriously? This is definitely not what Griff and I ordered for our reception dinner; that's for darn tootin'.

Waving from across the reception hall, I catch Von Cartier's attention.

He shrugs while giving me an odd look, not understanding what I'm trying to say from across the room.

I point to one of the reception dinner plates.

His eyes nearly pop from their sockets when what's on the plates registers, causing him to promptly faint.

When a plate of food is set down in front of Mrs. Rowling-Sakowitz-Goldman-Barrows, she completely loses control. In her frustration, she starts throwing food and unleashing a barrage of profanities like I've never heard before, all directed at poor, unconscious Von Cartier. It's pretty pointless since she's venting her frustrations at an unconscious wedding planner incapable of understanding a word she's spewing.

Griff and I are helpless as our reception spirals into one colossal dumpster fire after another. Despite our best efforts, we cannot prevent these unfortunate events from occurring. However, rather than losing our fuckin' minds, we surrender to the chaos and make the most of it, thanks to kind friends who generously share their marijuana with Griff and me.

The gay attendees love the festivities, wholeheartedly embracing the lively atmosphere as if attending a massive indoor picnic. They're going with the flow, having an absolute blast, and feeling like they are on top of the world. However, it's an entirely different story for the high-faluten-rich guests invited by Mrs. Rowling-Sakowitz-Goldman-Barrows. They're fleeing the reception in mass, looking much like the passengers and crew of the Titanic, desperately scrambling to escape a sinking ship. The scene would be complete if a small string orchestra performed "Nearer, My God, to Thee."

Looking back, who could've predicted things would go so wrong? I mean, seriously, it's like the universe was waiting for the perfect moment to pounce and screw with us. And let me tell you, it definitely delivered. Right from the start of this ordeal, Mr. Von Cartier had to deal with the never-ending demands of Mrs. Rowling-Sakowitz-Goldman-Barrows, all while trying to navigate Griff's and my many requests. But hey, somehow, he managed to keep Griff's secret from Mrs. Rowling-Sakowitz-Goldman-Barrows and sorted out the whole *best-man* situation when I ended up with an extra one. It was sad witnessing a once highly respected wedding planner reduced to a sniveling, unemployed gay queen.

Our troubles didn't stop there—no siree, Bob. Even more surprises were in store for us. The bakery delivered the wrong cake. I mean, seriously? We looked forward to our magnificent six-tiered Lemon Champagne cake, complete with an adorable pair of plastic *grooms* on top. But what did we end up with? A sad four-layered, flavorless, crummy, white cake with a plastic bride and groom cake topper that looked like it came out of an old breeder wedding magazine. It was horrible.

And if that wasn't enough, our orchestra didn't show. Their bus broke down just outside of town. Talk about bad mojo. But hey, we didn't let that ruin our party. Our excellent DJ kept the dance floor jumping with all the latest and greatest dance tunes.

So, despite the pink crêpe paper decorations, the hot dogs, the cake fiasco, and the missing orchestra, we still had an enjoyable time at our reception. Of course, I give the ample amounts of marijuana most of the credit for making the situation tolerable.

As the event drew to a close, I noticed that Mrs. Rowling-Sakowitz-Goldman-Barrows had vanished without a trace. She hadn't even bothered to congratulate us. Now that I think about it, I don't recall her exchanging a single word with Griff either. And to add to the disappointment, I still hadn't met my new almost-but-not-legal-mother-in-law.

Amidst the chaos of our commitment ceremony and reception, there was a glimmer of hope when something actually went according to plan–the liquor arrived just as we had ordered. With an abundance of top-shelf booze, plenty of pot, and incredible music, what more could a crowd of partying gays ask for at an unforgettable gay bash? It came as a shock to discover that our commitment ceremony and reception was the unexpected social event of the season, as quoted by the local gay community rag.

Oh, and you won't believe what happened to Kip. As the reception was winding down, Kip was wasted and hit on one of the State Police officers, and together, they disappeared for a while (if you get my drift). When the two emerged again, Kip wore handcuffs because he'd willingly surrendered himself to that very same officer (or maybe they got a little kinky). Kip was so wasted he had no clue what he was doing. But hey, he had a blast before being hauled back to prison. I bet it was days before he wiped that silly grin off his face.

I suppose the takeaway is that the ceremony isn't the focus of a commitment ceremony or wedding. It's really all about the love shared between the featured couple. Oh, and having generous friends who are totally cool with sharing their primo marijuana is a huge bonus.

* * *

Dale Thele

PART THREE

SO
LONG

Dale Thele

FINAL CHAPTERS

Wednesday, November 28, 1984

"Never say goodbye
because goodbye means going away
and going away means forgetting."

~ J.M. Barrie (*Peter Pan*) ~

The year is 1984. Ronald Reagan is reelected US president. Computer maker Apple released the first Mac, appropriately named after the Macintosh apple. You can fill your gas tank for $1.10 per gallon. A brand new 1984 Chevy Corvette costs $23,000. Milk is $2.26 per gallon, and a box of Rice Krispies costs $1.89. Prince's "When Doves Cry" tops the charts. Other hit singles include "What's Love Got to Do with It" by Tina Turner, "Footloose" by Kenny Loggins, and "Jump" by Van Halen. The movie *Ghostbusters* wins the year at the Box Office. Topping the appetizer menus are hollowed-out baked potato skins filled with cheese, bacon, and chives (with sour cream dip).

It's been over a year since Griff and I tied the knot at our commitment ceremony. Finally, after a year, we're preparing for our much-anticipated honeymoon. Our hectic work schedules prevented us from taking our well-deserved vacation earlier, but it's better late than never. Am I right?
After months of careful planning, we finally set a firm date for our late honeymoon. We're thrilled because everything is falling perfectly into place. And if you know me, you'll instantly guess where we're going.
I'll give you a hint: this place has been on my mind since I was a kid. If you still haven't figured it out, I'm talking about

209

none other than Disney World.

Now, I know what you're probably thinking. Disney World? Isn't that a place for kids? Well, let me tell you, my friend, Disney World is where dreams come true, no matter how old you are. From the enchanted castle to the thrilling rides, there's something for everyone to enjoy. And let's be honest, who won't miss the opportunity to meet Mickey Mouse in person?

We're thrilled to be preparing for our highly anticipated adventure. We can't wait to dive headfirst into the enchanting world of Disney, where we'll make unforgettable memories that will stay with us forever. This honeymoon will be like no other, and we're ready to grab hold of every magical moment that comes our way.

When I was a kid, Momma, Daddy, and I had a weekly ritual of gathering around the TV every Sunday evening to watch *The Wonderful World of Disney* show. It was our family thing, you know? But then there were those times during my summer vacation when I'd have to spend a whole week at my grandma's farm. Let me tell you, my grandma was a serious Bible-thumper. She didn't just go to Sunday school; she sat through the sermon and attended vesper services every Sunday and Wednesday evenings. And guess what? Those Sunday vesper services were always held at the same time as Walt Disney's show on TV. Can you sense the frustration I felt? I tried every excuse to avoid going to those vesper services, but my grandma was no fool. She saw right through my fake illnesses and tricks. So, as you can probably guess, those few Sunday evenings at Grandma's farm were anything but enjoyable for me.

However, most Sundays, I'd be at home with my parents. I always finished my chores and homework early, bathed, and prepared for Monday morning in advance to watch Mr. Disney's TV show.

I vividly remember this one time when Mr. Walt Disney appeared in person, no less, on TV. He was super pumped as he told of his grand plan of building a brand-spanking new theme park in Florida, which he planned to call Disney World. Excited, he showed sketches and miniature-to-scale models of this incredible future amusement park that would one day become a reality.

I asked my daddy if we could go to Disney World once it opened.

We'll see, he said, neither giving a resounding *yes* nor a definitive *no*. My heart raced with anticipation, and that's when I began to daydream about visiting Disney World. The mere thought of seeing the Magic Castle, meeting Mickey Mouse, and experiencing the thrilling Tea Cup ride excited me.

Week after week, I'd eagerly tune in to the Sunday evening TV program, filled with excitement and anticipation, just to see Mr. Disney. I couldn't wait to see him on the screen to give an update on the progress of Disney World. Occasionally, he'd announce something new and thrilling about his dream theme park. Those updates only fueled my already overflowing excitement to visit Disney World.

Years went by, and finally, Disney World opened to the public. However, to my disappointment, Daddy never took us there. Instead, we packed our imitation Airstream travel trailer and took a road trip to Six Flags Over Texas. Daddy tried to convince me that Six Flags was just as awesome, if not awesomer, than Disney World. But deep down, I knew there was no comparison between the two theme parks. Disney World existed on a whole other level, a gazillion times more extraordinary. It was a place of pure magic and wonder that I yearned to explore.

As I got older, my longing to visit Disney World became a life goal. Later, it evolved into the ultimate destination for my dream honeymoon, should I ever find the man of my dreams.

CHAPTER 1

Wednesday morning, November 28
Griff's and my condo

Like I said, Griff and I've nailed down a date for our much-anticipated honeymoon. We've got our hotel reservations and plane tickets all sorted out. Although we still need to pack our bags, we have nearly a whole month before leaving. On December 23rd, we'll hop on a direct flight to Florida. Once we touch down, we'll check into our Disney hotel. We'll celebrate Christmas and New Year's at Disney World, famously known as the most magical place on earth. We seriously can't wait to soak up all the joy and wonder this incredible destination offers.

The only thing that might mess up our plans is this annoying chest and head cold that's bugged me since before Thanksgiving. It's been a real pain in the neck and won't go away. I've tried every over-the-counter medicine and home remedy, but nothing seems to work. I feel absolutely terrible today, and I'm even concerned I might have a fever. I've been dealing with a stuffy nose, congestion, scratchy throat, and fatigue for weeks.

And to make matters worse, our trip is less than a month away. I'm hoping I'll be back to myself by then. I have to be, right?

Even though I'm feeling lousy, I've got a ton of errands I need to complete before our trip. This list is not in order:

- must shop for new clothes for our Florida vacation.
- write Christmas cards and send them out in the mail.
- buy gifts for the boys. I can't let them down. They have to have presents under the tree.

- racking my brain, trying to figure out what to get Griff for Christmas.
- got to take the boys to pick out a Christmas tree.

This never-ending to-do list is giving me a splitting headache, or maybe it's just the congestion in my head. I feel like I'm drowning in a sea of thoughts and snot swirling around.

All of a sudden, I snap back to reality. I'm in my kitchen, having coffee at the breakfast bar.

"Uncle Shane?" I barely hear through the fog clouding my mind. "Uncle Shane?" I hear again. The haze starts to clear. It hits me: Dexter is trying to get my attention.

He's sitting on a stool right beside me.

I'm cupping a mug of lukewarm coffee as my mind wanders in a thick pea-soup-like fog.

"Uncle Shane," he says. "Are you feeling alright? You look totally zoned out, like you're in outer space."

"I'm fine," I say, shaking my head to clear my mind. But let's face it, a slight head shaking doesn't do much to relieve the congestion in my noggin. Instead, it makes everything worse. The sudden movement throws me off balance. I grab Dexter's arm to prevent my toppling off the breakfast bar stool.

"Uncle Shane?" Dexter asks, concern evident in his voice. "What's the matter?"

"Nothing to worry about, Dex," I reply with a forced smile. "It's just this darn cold. I can't seem to shake it, you know?" I release his arm, not wanting to alarm the kid, even though I must admit, I feel like death warmed over. Desperately seeking support, I lean against the kitchen counter, hoping to regain my stability.

"You're not okay," Dexter insists.

"Give me a moment. It'll pass," I say, attempting to reassure both of us. "I'll be okay." I grip my coffee mug with both hands, but it trembles uncontrollably. The coffee inside ripples like a tiny earthquake rattling inside the ceramic container.

"Uncle Shane," Dexter says, his voice filled with worry.

"You're scaring me. I'm taking you to the Emergency Room."

"No, there's no need for that," I reply, unsure if I'm trying to convince him or myself. I don't want Dexter to be burdened with worrying about me.

Feeling woozy, I grab Dexter's arm for support.

He catches me before I fall off the stool.

My favorite ceramic mug slips through my hands. I watch it tumble in slow motion to crash land on the floor, shattering into sharp shards and splattering coffee on my clean kitchen floor. My emotions are everywhere, and my eyes start to water. I try to reassure myself that it's just spilled coffee and a broken mug, nothing to get emotional about. But still, the salty tears fill my eyes as emotions bubble to the surface.

"Maybe you're right," I say, looking through watery eyes at the mess I've made on the floor. Then, I turn my attention to Dexter's concerned gaze. "Dex, could you take me to the hospital?"

Dexter assists me into an empty chair in the busy hospital emergency waiting room before he heads to the front desk to check me in. I feel guilty for inconveniencing Dexter for dragging me here. I'm feeling much better now, but guilt tugs at me as I look around at the folks who need a doctor more urgently than I do. They're bundled in blankets, wearing heavy winter coats, while coughing, sneezing, and wheezing. I'm suddenly concerned I might catch a nasty bug along with this annoying cold, especially in this germ-infested room.

Dexter comes back with a clipboard and check-in forms for me to complete. He begins bombarding me with questions from the papers.

I tell him I can complete the forms myself.

Reluctantly, he looks at me as if questioning my abilities before handing me the clipboard and ballpoint pen. He settles in the chair beside me.

Out of the corner of my eye, I notice him looking around the waiting room, which is filled with very sick people. He sinks into the chair and pulls his turtleneck sweater over his mouth and nose.

Once I finish completing the paperwork, I get up from the chair, intending to walk to the check-in desk to return the clipboard.

"No, Uncle Shane," Dexter says, grabbing hold of my arm, his voice filled with concern. "Sit back down. I'll return the forms."

"Dex, I appreciate your concern, but I can handle this," pulling from his loose grip on my arm.

"Okay," Dexter replies, worry still evident on his face.

"Will you please stop worrying?" I say.

Dexter shrugs and remains silent.

Ignoring his silence, I walk to the check-in counter.

The lady behind the counter examines the paperwork like a school teacher grading a paper, scanning each detail.

"Everything seems to be in order," she says, checking both sides of the forms. "May I see your insurance card?"

I reach for the wallet in my hip pocket...

CHAPTER 2

Friday morning, December 7
Hospital Room

Waking up, I discover my eyelashes are glued together with that crusty gunk that accumulates on lashes during sleep. After some struggle, I can open my eyes and look around at my surroundings. Let me tell you, I'm clueless as to where I am. Everything is unfamiliar and hazy, thanks to the remnants of sleep clouding my vision.

Blinking a few times, I hope to clear my sight, but no luck. A smoky halo is happening around the edges of my vision. I try to move my arm and realize it's tangled in tubes and wires connected to machines, making all sorts of clicking and swooshing noises. It's as if the devices are trying to amplify the eerie silence in the room. I attempt to move my other arm to find it tethered to hoses and wires. I'm bound, completely immobile, and my field of vision is limited, too.

From what I can tell, I'm in a fairly spacious room. Maybe a conference room, minus the table and chairs. The bed I'm lying on and the machines surrounding me create a little island in the middle of a vast emptiness. Oh, and there's a slightly ajar door on the other side of the room. I vaguely make out what looks like a toilet in the darkness. I'm not sure about anything right now. My vision fades in and out, making it difficult to focus on any one thing for long.

Scanning the room, I see another door open. A figure enters the room. I can't determine if this person is male or female because they're covered head-to-toe in a protective jumpsuit. As they come closer, I catch what appears to be brown eyes, partially lined with flaking mascara, peering through foggy safety goggles.

"Can you tell me where I am?" I ask, feeling confused and frustrated.

The person says nothing; they are more interested in fiddling with hoses and wires and adjusting knobs on the machines. It's as if I don't even exist. Talk about rude, huh? Then again, maybe they're deaf or don't understand English.

So, I'm lying in a hospital-type bed. At the same time, a stranger wearing blue latex gloves messes with hoses and wires connected to me, attached to machines surrounding the bed. The person seems to know what they're doing, but who are they? What are they doing to me? I'm utterly defenseless in this situation. Once they finish whatever they're up to, they walk toward the door without saying a word. As the door opens, I catch sight of red plastic streamers hanging on the other side. I may not be a genius, but even I know that colored streamers have different meanings. So, what the heck does red signify? And then it comes me—danger. What on earth could lurk on the other side of that door that's so darn dangerous?

I rack my brain, trying to recall the last thing I remember before falling asleep. But wait, I don't remember falling asleep. What's with the red streamers? And why did that person come into this room wearing all that protective gear? Maybe I'm just dreaming. Yeah, that's got to be it. This whole situation feels like a messed-up nightmare. My eyelids become heavy and flutter shut.

I'm jolted awake by a different person standing beside my bed; they are also wearing a protective jumpsuit. They're flipping through papers attached to a clipboard.

"Hello, young man," a male voice emits through a face mask. "My name is Doctor Carlton. Can you verify your full name?"

"Shane Aaron Davison," I reply, groggy and wondering if this is real or just another dream.

"Tell me, what day it is?" he asks.

"Sure," I pause before replying, "Wednesday, November 28, 1984."

"I see," the hooded man nods. "What would you say if I told you today is Friday, December 7th?"

"What?" I say, jerking up in the bed.

"Easy there, cowboy," he coaxes, gently guiding my upper body back into a reclining position. "You've been in a coma for nine days," he calmly says.

Confusion consumes me as I gaze at the masked face in utter disbelief. The protective suit conceals all details except for dark eyes peering through safety goggles, which momentarily fog over with each breath.

"Where am I?" I ask the doctor.

"You're in St. Joseph's Hospital," he says.

"I don't understand," I press on for answers. "How did I get here?"

"You experienced an unfortunate episode and collapsed while checking in at the emergency center," he says. "You have no memory of the incident?"

"I remember waking up earlier when someone came into the room and fiddled with the tubes and machines," I say.

"But you don't recall coming to the hospital?" the doctor asks.

I shake my head and take a moment to let everything sink in, pausing to let what I've learned play back in my head.

The doctor scribbles on papers clipped to a clipboard.

"So, let me get this straight," I say, "I collapsed nine days ago while checking in at the ER. I've been in a coma. And now, I'm a patient at St. Joseph's Hospital. Is that correct?"

"Yes, that's correct," the man nods.

"Why am I here? What's wrong with me?"

The man clears his throat, hesitates momentarily, and then delivers the news.

"Young man," the doctor says. "You have full-blown AIDS."

His words hit me hard, and I struggle to process them.

AIDS? Me? Impossible. This isn't happening to me. Not to me.

The doctor continues spewing complicated medical jargon

that flies over my head. It's as if he's speaking a foreign language, and to understand what he's saying requires the help of a translator.

I want Griff, I think to myself. *Where's Griff?*

As my thoughts and internal questions make sense, I grasp fragments of the doctor's explanation when he simplifies his terms. Yet, phrases echo in my head, like:

"Possibly, you have two months, at best..."

"You have options..."

"Stay here or go home—if you have someone to care for you..."

"Get your affairs in order..."

"The decision is yours to make..."

All the while, I'm struggling to make sense of the situation and understand the gravity of my condition while also grappling with the shock of what has transpired.

A tear rolls down my cheek.

Where's Griff? I need Griff...

CHAPTER 3

Monday late morning, December 10. 1984
Griff's and my condo

After enduring a challenging ten-day hospital stay, returning home is a relief. But things are different. Griff moved his stuff from our bedroom to the guest room during my absence. He put our king-size bed in storage because the guest room accommodates up to a queen bed. All of this to make room for a rented hospital-type bed for me. Our previously shared bedroom became what Griff called my *recovery room*.

But wait, I'm getting ahead of myself. Let's go back to when Griff brought me home on Monday. You see, I wasn't exactly in the best of moods; my new medications were disagreeing with me. Let's say my body rejected the prescribed medications. As if that wasn't enough, I was too weak to walk without assistance. I felt like crap, and the moment Griff wheeled me into the condo, I broke down and cried. During my hospital stay, I'd held myself together. But once I was home, I couldn't hold back any longer. I don't know if it was the realization of what it meant to have AIDS. Or the uncertainty of the future. Maybe it was the relief to be home and in a familiar setting. Whatever the reason, the tears flowed as Griff held me. We had a good long cry for different reasons.

After a while, when both of us were cried out, Griff wheeled me into the *recovery room*. He hadn't warned me beforehand about the modifications to our bedroom, but I understood the reasoning behind it. I didn't put up a fight, basically because I didn't have the strength to argue with him. He'd been assertive with the hospital doctor, emphasizing his opposition to placing me in hospice. In so doing, Griff had to make changes at the condo to accommodate my current needs. I was grateful to Griff; he was there for me to handle the details I was too ill to attend to.

My rearranged bedroom was adorned with cut flower arrangements and live blooming plants. Each piece of furniture with space was covered with lovely floral arrangements.

I received a bunch of get-well cards. I recognized familiar names of people who had never bothered sending Christmas cards. But here, they sent get-well cards as if they cared. Cards came from neighbors I'd never met or wouldn't recognize if we passed in the hall or elevator. It's like they suddenly cared about me now that they know I'm seriously ill. It makes you wonder. And it put things into perspective.

Griff had my back when I was in the hospital, ensuring my every need was handled. He followed Dr. Carlton's instructions to a T and even dealt with the whole hospital checkout process. Man, those final few days in the hospital felt like they'd never end. I couldn't have visitors. It was as if I was in prison. I stayed connected with Griff and the boys over the phone, but not seeing them in person made me miss them even more.

One factor that made my hospital stay feel like an eternity was the medications they gave me. Unfortunately, the meds made me sick, which seriously messed with my sleep. As a result, I couldn't keep food down and had to rely on an IV tube for nutrition. Sadly, my condition hasn't improved, and I've still got an IV in my arm for sustenance. On the plus side, I'm allowed small amounts of water, clear juice, and crushed ice as a treat—as long as I'm a good boy.

The specialized bed Griff rented from a hospital supply store is much more comfortable than the one I had during my hospital stay. Moreover, the sheets he put on this bed are of higher quality, so they don't feel like the scratchy sandpaper sheets I had to endure during my hospital confinement. I'm thrilled to have my goose-down bed pillows back. Those flat, pancake-like things the hospital called *pillows* were an embarrassment to pillows everywhere.

I'm not thrilled about being stuck in bed, but I've accepted that it's for my safety. I'm considered a *fall risk*. I found this out the hard way when I tried to make a solo trip to the bathroom while in the hospital. I managed to scoot my way to the edge of the bed with my legs dangling over the side. I lowered my legs slowly until my feet touched the freezing linoleum floor. As I attempted to stand, my legs buckled, and I crashed to the floor. I have no idea how long I lay there on that icy, unforgiving, hard-tiled floor before someone found me. Luckily, I'd managed to grab the blanket from the bed and wrap myself as best I could. But let me tell you, that thin blanket did little to shield me from the freezing floor.

Someone eventually found me shivering on the cold tile floor and called for assistance. Two burly orderlies swooped in and hoisted me back into bed. Since then, I've not attempted to get out of bed without help. Besides, safety rails have been raised on my bed, making me feel as if I'm a caged animal inside my bed. But I understand it's for my own good.

Looking back to when I was stuck on that freezing floor, I noticed how scrawny my legs had become. I checked my arms; they were thinner than I remembered. Then, I realized my earlier desire to look in a mirror wasn't as strong as I had first hoped. I felt like a mere skeleton wrapped in rubbery skin. It made me wonder what other changes had taken place within me since I first arrived at the hospital. I recall reading somewhere that people who contract AIDS kind of waste away overnight. Is that what's happening to me?

CHAPTER 4

Saturday morning, December 15
my bedroom

Waking, I open my eyes to soak in the tranquility. The sun's rays beat against the closed curtains, hinting it's probably late morning. I keep the drapes shut because my eyes have recently become sensitive to bright light. It's funny how I used to take simple things like seeing the sun for granted. Now, I find myself avoiding the sun. Instead, I stare at the ceiling, lost in thoughts about what the day has in store for me, just like I've done almost every morning. Then reality slaps me upside the head— I'm sick, and I remember my entire day will be another battle for survival—to make it through one more day.

A sad, warm tear crawls down my cheek.

Moments later, a gentle latex-gloved hand dabs it away with a soft tissue.

Pivoting my head on the pillow, I expect to see Griff's masked face. But to my surprise, it's Cal standing beside my bed, his face partially concealed behind a protective mask. Even with the cover, I recognize him.

Man, talk about a whirlwind of emotions. Just seeing Cal brings tears of joy streaming down my face. I can't help it; they keep coming. It feels like an eternity since I last laid eyes on him, even though it's only been a little over a year since Griff's and my commitment ceremony. When I was in the hospital, I was afraid I'd not see Cal again.

"Cal," I say, my voice trembling. "What are you doing here?"

"Griff phoned me," Cal explains. "Why didn't you let me know sooner?""I only just recently found out," I reply, my eyes welling with another wave of tears.

"When I heard the news, I immediately hopped on a plane," Cal exclaims.

Due to Cal's unexpected arrival, I gather Griff told him about my limited time. I don't want our conversation to turn into a pity party, you know? I want to make the most of the time I have left.

"Is there anything you want or need?" Cal asks.

"Well, I want a new, uninfected body. However, for now, I'll settle for some juice."

"Sure thing, buddy," Cal responds, then leaves the room.

Cal has barely left when Griff enters.

"Good morning, sunshine," Griff greets me with a smile, his voice slightly muffled by his face mask. The doctor insists everyone around me wear protective gear, so Griff wears a face mask and latex gloves.

The face masks and gloves are intended to shield me from the everyday germs that may not threaten an otherwise healthy person. However, even a single airborne germ or virus could spell disaster for someone in my weakened condition.

"What time is it?" I inquire.

"It's almost lunchtime," Griff says.

"What?" I protest. "Why did you let me sleep so late?"

"You were sleeping so peacefully—I didn't want to disturb you," he shrugs. "Besides, you haven't had such a restful sleep since you returned home."

"Did you feed the boys this morning?" I ask, knowing Dexter and Joshua regularly show up to mooch breakfast.

"It's Saturday," Griff replies. "On the weekends, the boys come for lunch—not breakfast. They'll be here soon."

"That's right," I say, unsure of what I'm agreeing to. Man, I tell you, keeping my days in order is like trying to untangle a bunch of cooked spaghetti. They mush together, running into each other without clear boundaries. I swear, the harder I try to keep track of the days, the more I mess things up. Time is precious, and I'm painfully aware I don't have much of it. But somehow, it keeps slipping through my fingers with each passing day.

"When did Cal get here?" I ask, feeling disoriented.

"He arrived yesterday evening," Griff says, looking at me curiously. "Don't you remember visiting with him?"

Searching the fragmented pieces of my memories, I have no recollection of spending time with Cal, not since our commitment ceremony—a year ago.

Is Griff pulling my leg? No, he wouldn't prank me.

"Oh, right," I nod, not wanting to worry Griff more than I probably already am. However, I don't recall seeing Cal before this morning.

Cal returns with a plastic-lidded cup of apple juice with a straw sticking out from the top.

"How did you know I wanted apple juice?" I ask Cal.

Cal starts to say something, but Griff abruptly interrupts him, lightly touching his arm and shaking his head. It's evident to me what's going on. Griff protects my dignity by not permitting Cal to notice my declining memory. I don't say anything, not wanting to stir up additional problems. I must have requested apple juice during our evening visit since Cal knew my preference. Still, I have no recollection of yesterday evening.

CHAPTER 5

Saturday afternoon, December 15
my bedroom

The afternoon and evening are spent with Dexter, Joshua, Cal, Griff, and some drop-in guests. It's a crazy day, meeting people whose names I can't recall or remember how I know them. But hey, they smile and freely chat as if we've been friends forever.

The guests tell entertaining stories that involve me. Stories I don't remember ever happening. Cal tells some whoppers from when he and I went to high school together. His stories crack everyone up; they're absolute blasts to listen to. I must admit, I love listening to his tales, even though I wasn't a part of them in real life. Cal is being Cal, adding me to his stories to make me feel like I'm a part of something bigger than myself. In high school, he always ensured I felt like I belonged, even when I was the odd man out.

"There was this one time," Cal begins, leaning back in his chair, a mischievous glint in his eyes. "Shane and I decided to pull off a daring escapade—breaking into the high school principal's office. You see, ol' man Gardner—our principal— had it out for Shane ever since he first started attending senior high school."

"Why on earth would you break into the principal's office?" Dexter asks.

"Well," Cal chuckles, his voice tinged with excitement. "Your uncle and I suspected someone had tampered with his senior grades. We came up with a plan to sneak into the school office one night and ensure they hadn't been altered."

"Had they been changed?" Joshua asks.

"Just as we suspected," Cal affirms with a nod. "The grades on your uncle's permanent record had indeed been altered.

Someone used liquid correction fluid to cover the original grades and replace them with lower marks."

"Who'd do something like that?" Dexter asks.

"We suspected ol' man Gardner," Cal says.

"Gardner must have been a real jerk," Joshua says.

"Oh, trust me," Cal says, "he definitely was. From when your uncle was a sophomore, Gardner was constantly on your uncle's case."

"What did Uncle Shane do to piss him off?" Dexter asks.

"Well, that's a long story," Cal says casually. "One we'll save for another time."

"So, what happened to Uncle Shane's grades? Did they get fixed?" Dexter asks.

"Yep," Cal replies with a wide grin. "I changed them back to their original state."

"You didn't get caught?" Joshua asks.

"We came close," Cal admits. "After fixing your uncle's grades, we heard voices one floor below us."

"Oh no!" Dexter gasps.

"What did you do?" Joshua asks.

"I told your uncle to quietly sneak downstairs through the auditorium using the backstage stairs and hide in the theater department costume room," Cal explains.

"Why that room?" Dexter asks.

"Let me tell you, your uncle practically took up residence in that room during his three-year stint in the drama club," Cal says. "He reorganized and cleaned that room. In doing so, Shane knew every nook and cranny like the back of his hand. I figured he could effortlessly blend in with the hanging costumes and vanish without a trace. No one would have stood a chance of finding him in that maze of costumes."

"But what about you, Uncle Cal?" Joshua inquires. "How did you keep from getting caught?"

"Oh, it was a piece of cake," Cal shrugs. "I diverted the cop's attention, ensuring they were too preoccupied with me to even consider searching for your uncle. Plus, it was the dead of night;

there weren't any lights, and they had no clue how many of us they were hunting for in that dark school building."

"So, what happened?" Joshua asks.

"Well," Cal resumes, "I kept the cops on their toes by leading them on a wild goose chase through the building. Once I had the perfect opportunity, I quietly slipped out of the building, hoping your uncle would do the same when he had a clear shot to escape."

"Interesting," Dexter interjects. "Then what happened?"

"The following afternoon," Cal continues, "your uncle and I met at the city park across from the high school. We laughed like crazy over the absurdity of what happened overnight."

"Did you and Uncle Shane hang out a lot during high school?" Joshua asks.

"Well, I suppose you could say we hung out pretty regularly," Cal responds. "There was this one time when I found out that your uncle had never been to a football game."

"No way!" Dexter exclaims, his eyes go wide.

"That's right," Cal chuckles, shaking his head, "can you believe it? I figured it was high time he experienced the thrill of a live high school football game, just like any other teenager. You know, back in the day, football was everything to me. I was the star quarterback of our high school."

"Of course," Dexter smirks. "Uncle Cal will never let us forget that."

Cal shoots Dexter a playful side-eye with a mischievous glint in his eyes.

"Ah, but let me tell you what I did to rectify the situation," Cal says. "Picture this: it was a Sunday night, around 10 o'clock. The football field was deserted, not a soul around. It was just the two of us. The field was engulfed in darkness, except for the glow of the almost full moon. I tossed a football to your uncle. He just stood there, frozen in place. The ball smacked him in the chest, not too hard, but enough to make him flinch."

" 'Duffus,' I told Shane, 'when a ball comes whizzing at you,

you're to catch it and toss it back.'

" 'I've never played ball,' he told me.

" 'Didn't you play catch with your dad, you know, when you were a kid?' I asked him.

" 'Nope. My daddy never wanted to do that kind of stuff with me,' he confessed.

"That's when it hit me. It was high time your uncle Shane learned the basics of the game. I took it upon myself to teach him how to catch and throw. He caught on pretty well, but it was clear he wouldn't be recruited by any college teams. However, that wasn't the point. The objective was for him to grasp the fundamentals of football before attending his first game.

"The first lesson was cut short when the automatic sprinklers came on, spraying water everywhere. We ran off the field, laughing our fool heads off.

"Anyway, the very next Friday, your uncle tagged along with my girlfriend, Cat, to his first-ever football game," Cal recounts with a hint of excitement.

"Wait a minute," Dexter interjects, "you had a girlfriend?"

"Yeah, believe it or not," Cal responds with a chuckle. "But our relationship kinda fizzled after about a year."

"What led to the breakup?" Joshua asks.

"Well," Cal takes a moment to gather his thoughts before answering, "our split was sort of mutual, you know?"

"No way, Uncle Cal," Joshua insists. "You're not getting off the hook that easy. How come you two called it quits?"

"Alright," Cal sighs. "If you really must know, Cat somehow figured out I was into guys. It wasn't something we'd talked about."

"Wait, you weren't out?" Dexter blurts.

"No," Cal replies. "It's sort of complicated. As the star high school quarterback, people had certain expectations of me."

"You mean they expected you to be straight?" Dexter clarifies.

"Yeah, exactly," Cal agrees. "But Cat saw right through my

act and called me out on it."

"So, you're saying she outed you?" Dexter asks.

"Kind of," Cal replies. "She respected me enough not to publicly out me. When we were alone, she dropped subtle hints, letting me know she suspected I wasn't as straight as I pretended to be. And that led to us breaking up."

"I'm sorry, Uncle Cal," Dexter says sympathetically.

"It's all water under the bridge now," Cal says. "What was I blabbering about before I was sidetracked?"

"You were telling us about Uncle Shane and his first football game," Joshua interjects.

"Oh yeah," Cal says, "your uncle attended his first high school football game. He saw a real game in action and watched me do my thing on the football field."

More stories about Cal followed, accompanied by lots of laughs and even a few tears. Cal had a captive audience and made the most of it—he loved the attention.

Joshua and Dexter follow after Cal with stories about themselves and me. Witnessing how effortlessly they finish each other's sentences is fascinating. It's like their tales are more than just made-up stories, and the lengths they went to make it seem I played a significant role in their narratives.

"When Dex was in the hospital after being beaten up by a gang of bullies in high school," Joshua says, nodding towards Dexter, "I went to visit him in the hospital."

"I hated my hospital room," Dexter adds. "It had a weird smell."

"Really? You never mentioned that to me," Joshua says, sounding surprised.

"You never asked," Dexter snickers. "Go on with your story. Which visit are you talking about when you came to see me? You came almost every day."

"You'd only been in that second room for a short while. You can't expect me to remember the date—like you said, I was there almost every day."

"Yup, you were a regular," Dexter acknowledges. "Are you talking about the time when you thought you were responsible for me getting hurt and ended up in the hospital?"

"Yeah," Joshua confirms. "That's when I first met Uncle Shane."

"I remember introducing you," Dexter recalls. "Uncle Shane was visiting me, and you came into the room."

"That's right, you introduced me to your uncle," Joshua affirms.

"Seems so long ago, now," Dexter says. "We've gone through a lot since then."

"We most definitely have," Joshua agrees. "But you know what? If I had to do things differently, I wouldn't change a thing. I'm happy with how everything turned out."

"Me too," Dexter adds. "Me too."

Dexter and Joshua told countless stories about themselves and me. Unfortunately, I didn't recall ever being a part of their tales in real life. Griff, on the other hand, joined in when the boys ran out of stories to tell. He shared the most captivating story about how he and I first met. Honestly, I don't remember how we met. Nonetheless, his story was charming, even if he made it up to make me feel good.

"Shane and I connected through a personals ad in the newspaper," Griff said. "Little did I know that Josh and Dex had placed the ad to assist Shane in finding a boyfriend."

"But Griff," Dexter interjects, "you and Uncle Shane had already met before that personals ad."

"Yes, that's true," Griff says. "We had met, and yet we hadn't. Our initial meeting took place at a costume ball. Regrettably, we didn't see each other's faces due to the masks we wore. Despite the veil of anonymity, we shared a few dances. I found myself inexplicably drawn to the mysterious man, even though I knew nothing about him—not even his name."

"So what happened?" Cal asks.

"Uncle Cal?" Dexter asks. "You haven't heard the whole story, have you?"

"I guess I haven't," says Cal.

"Well," Griff says, "between dances, I decided to get some punch for the both of us, and when I returned, the enigmatic gentleman vanished into thin air."

"Hold on a second," Cal interrupts. "Where do the personals ad come in?"

"I'm getting to that," Griff says. "It wasn't long after the fundraiser that I found a personals ad in the newspaper. It led me to Shane, and we went on a dinner date. The funny thing is, neither of us recognized each other from the masquerade ball."

"Ah, right! The masks from the ball threw you off," Joshua chimes in.

"Yeah, exactly," Griff agrees. "But let me tell you, that dinner date was incredible. I had such an amazing time and was looking forward to going out with Shane again. Our date hadn't even ended, and I had already planned to call him the next day."

"But you didn't call," Joshua points out.

"Nope, I didn't," Griff admits. "Unknowingly, I'd dropped the card with Shane's number while we were having dinner. And then, after we left the restaurant, unknown to me, Shane returned to get the business card case he had accidentally left on the table. That's when he found the card he had given me—it was lying on the floor beside the table where we'd had our dinner."

"Uncle Shane assumed you weren't interested in seeing you again," Dexter chimes in.

"Yeah, that's pretty much how it went down," Griff nods. "But then, by pure happenstance, we bumped into each other again when I responded to a maintenance call to fix a leaky pipe in Shane's bathroom. That's when the magic happened, and we reconnected."

"Griff," Dexter leans in and says, "I love hearing how you and Uncle Shane figured things out."

"Haven't you heard this story enough times?" Griff asks.

"No," Dexter says, "I can't hear the story enough. Please, tell it. Please?"

"Well, alright," Griff says, feigning reluctance. "How many times have you heard this story?"

"Honestly," Dexter says, his mischievous grin spreads across his face, revealing his delight. "I can never get tired of it."

"I haven't heard this part either," Cal says. "Please, do go on."

Griff settles comfortably into his chair, preparing to share the intriguing details.

"Alright then," Griff begins. "Like I said, I arrived at Shane's condo to fix a busted pipe. Little did I know, Shane had grown a stubble beard and was sporting eyeglasses."

"Exactly," Joshua adds. "When you and Uncle Shane met for your *personals ad* dinner, he looked completely different. He wore contact lenses and was clean-shaven."

"It had been months since our personals ad date," Griff adds. "But anyway, as I mentioned, I arrived at Shane's condo to repair a broken pipe. Shane took me to the master bath to the leak. I crawled halfway inside the vanity cabinet where the leaky pipe was. When I turned on the water valve to locate the source of the leak. I opened the valve too quickly, and I got sprayed with water. Thankfully, Shane came to the rescue, handed me a towel, and offered to dry my uniform shirt so I wouldn't have to spend the afternoon in a wet uniform."

An excited Dexter bounces in his chair as if he needs to wee.

"This is my favorite part of the story!" Dexter says.

"I innocently removed my shirt, catching Shane's attention. He spotted the chain around my neck and noticed something dangling from it—curious, he asked about the hanging item.

"I explained—it's a sterling silver initial pinkie ring.

"Shane's eyes sparkled with excitement, and he asked if he could have a closer look.

"I obliged, removing the chain, unfastening it, and handing him the ring.

"As Shane held the ring, he asked where I had gotten it. I told him I'd stumbled upon it at a charity event. At that moment, a wave of emotions crashed over Shane, overwhelming his senses. Memories surged, transporting him back to when we swayed together on the dance floor, sharing an unforgettable connection. The realization hit him with great force as he vividly recalled his sudden departure, leaving our encounter without a goodbye.

"In that very moment, an overwhelming certainty washed over me—I'd undoubtedly discovered the true owner of the ring. It was as if the universe had conspired to connect us through a piece of jewelry, a symbol of fate intertwining our lives."

"The way Uncle Shane and Griff crossed paths is like something from a fairy tale," Dexter chokes with emotion, eyes shimmering with joy as he swipes away a tear.

"We had a heartfelt conversation," Griff recounts with a smile. "Together, we unraveled the misunderstanding surrounding Shane's discovery of the business card I had accidentally dropped on the restaurant floor. And in that transformative moment, we looked deep into each other's eyes. When our lips met, I knew with absolute certainty that Shane was destined for me. The taste of Dentyne chewing gum lingered on his lips, sealing our connection."

"I know the Dentyne reference," Cal says. "That's Shane's favorite chewing gum."

The guests visited among themselves about the many stories they'd heard throughout the evening.

Not saying a word, Dexter left my bedroom.

Little did I know what was about to happen next. The most enchanting piano melody suddenly drifted into my room from the living room. It was slow and melancholy, as if each ivory key was carefully considered before being pressed. It had been ages since I last heard Dexter play, but I've always adored his music. A grand piano sits in the living room; as of late, it's become a dust collector. But now, the soothing tunes he plays bring tears to my eyes. Unbeknownst to him, Dexter's giving me the most incredible gift anyone has ever given me—the gift of his music.

The evening was entertaining; everyone had fun sharing stories that revolved around me. They laughed and had a great time. I found it amusing to listen to their tales, making me wonder if any of those stories even had a hint of truth to them.

The party broke up, and the guests left. Only a little later, Dexter and Joshua left the gathering to return to their apartment near the University while Cal went to his hotel.

It's just Griff and me in the condo.

Without the laughter and storytelling, my bedroom feels eerily empty. The folding chairs, once filled with guests who were here just a half hour ago, surround my bed, empty and lifeless.

Griff says *goodnight,* turns off the lights, and partially shuts the guest bedroom door, leaving the condo dark and silent.

Dexter's piano music lingers in my head.

Exhaustion washes over me, I feel my eyelids growing heavy.

There's nothing to bargain with for more time.

I've shared my final story to the best of my ability.

Now, like any good tale, mine must end.

The End

Shane Davison's sterling silver signet ring

Sneak Peek
at
the next novel
coming soon
by
Dale Thele

Ezekiel & Abrahim
GHOSTS of LOST CREEK JUNCTION
a fictional novel by

Dale Thele

Lost Creek Junction is a tiny Texas town with more ghosts than living, breathing folks. It's always been a small, quiet town. And let me tell ya, all the folks here were born and raised in these parts. They know everyone, all the local legends and the town's folklore like the back of their hand.

Now, picture this: one beautiful May morning, not long ago, a stranger named Taylor Elliott rolled into town on the morning train. And let me tell ya, trains hardly ever stop in Junction except to occasionally drop off or pick up folks. Because of that, Mr. Elliott became the talk of the town. On summer break from college, Taylor drags his bags down the dusty main street of Lost Creek Junction and heads straight to the vacant house of the late widow Blackburn. He walks in like he owns the place, and guess what? Turns out he actually inherited it. Now, the ownership of that house has been a head-scratcher almost since it was built. It's had more owners than probably any building standing in Junction. It changed hands three times through poker games, once due to checkers, and was twice confiscated by the county for unpaid taxes. But somehow, Mr. Elliott ended up with it, lock, stock, and barrel. No one around these parts knows how he's related to the ol' widow Blackburn (may she rest in peace). Still, he must be connected to her somehow to inherit such a big, fancy old house.

This is where things get interesting. Enter Ezekiel and Abrahim, two bitter rivals from way back. These rowdy and obnoxious scoundrels are enemies even after more than a century in the afterlife. As ghosts, they find themselves reigniting an ugly Hatfield and McCoy-type rivalry when the land they've fought over is awarded to Mr. Elliott. The residents of Lost Creek Junction, both alive and dead, join forces with Taylor to battle Ezekiel and Abrahim's ghostly shenanigans from destroying Lost Creek Junction forever.

Watch for the future release of
GHOSTS of LOST CREEK JUNCTION

About The Author

Most of Dale Thele's life has been a lengthy series of compulsions strung together by atrocious acts of stupidity due to boredom. After raising heck in a sleepy oil town in north-central Oklahoma for eighteen years, he ventured to Oklahoma City University on a quest for higher education. He quickly learned "higher" education meant to "elevate" one's mind with the aid of either a reefer or a bong, and ample amounts of alcohol. Some years later destiny dragged him to Austin, Texas, where he currently lives vicariously through the fictional characters he congers up, and the far-fetched adventures he writes.

Visit the Official Author Website:
www.DaleThele.com

LGBTQIA+ RESOURCES

The Trevor Project – www.thetrevorproject.org
TrevorLifeline – 1-866-488-7386
A non-profit organization focusing on suicide prevention efforts among lesbian, gay, bisexual, transgender, queer, and questioning (LGBTQ) youth. They also operate The Trevor Lifeline, a confidential service that offers trained counselors.

National Suicide Prevention Lifeline –
www.suicidepreventionlifeline.org
National Suicide Prevention Lifeline – 1-800-273-8255
A suicide prevention network of over 160 crisis centers providing 24/7 service via a toll-free hotline:
1-800-273-8255 (TALK)
It is available to anyone in suicidal crisis or emotional distress.

It Gets Better Project – www.itgetsbetter.org
An Internet-based nonprofit founded in response to the suicides of teenagers who were bullied because they were gay or because their peers suspected that they were gay. Its goal is to prevent suicide among LGBT youth by having gay adults convey the message that these teens' lives will improve.

PFLAG – www.pflag.org
The United States' first and largest organization uniting parents, families, and allies with people who are lesbian, gay, bisexual, transgender, and queer. PFLAG National is the national organization, which provides support to the PFLAG network of local chapters

Discover
Shane Davison Chronicles Series
from the beginning
(four book series)
Amazon Best Selling novel from
Dale Thele

Shane Davison reveals a poignant coming-of-age narrative of growing up in ultra-conservative, north-central Oklahoma in the early 1970s, told entirely from Shane's teenage perspective. From triumphs to disappointments, his story unravels a tapestry of secrets and lies, exposing deeply hidden skeletons in closets that should never see the light of day. A fictional novel, inspired by actual events.

Series includes: CLIPPED WINGS, BLURRED LINES, CHASING UNICORNS, and FINAL CHAPTERS

Other Titles by Dale Thele

Masked Identities

Roadhouse Friday

Harvest Moon

Naughty Gay Adult Bedtime Stories

Clipped Wings

Blurred Lines

Find these titles at
www.dalethele.com

www.ingramcontent.com/pod-product-compliance
Lightning Source LLC
Chambersburg PA
CBHW050723180626
46814CB00002B/571